www.**penguin**.co.uk

You Think It,
I'll Say It

By Curtis Sittenfeld

You Think It, I'll Say It
Eligible
Sisterland
American Wife
The Man of My Dreams
Prep

You Think It,
I'll Say It

Stories

Curtis Sittenfeld

Doubleday

LONDON · TORONTO · SYDNEY · AUCKLAND · JOHANNESBURG

TRANSWORLD PUBLISHERS
61–63 Uxbridge Road, London W5 5SA
www.penguin.co.uk

Transworld is part of the Penguin Random House group of companies
whose addresses can be found at global.penguinrandomhouse.com

Penguin
Random House
UK

First published in Great Britain in 2018 by Doubleday
an imprint of Transworld Publishers

The following stories in this collection have been previously published,
sometimes in a different form: 'The Nominee' in *Esquire* (US), 'Gender Studies'
and 'The Prairie Wife' in the *New Yorker* and 'Bad Latch' in the *Washington Post
Magazine*. In addition, 'A Regular Couple' was published as a Kindle Single in
partnership with the *Atlantic*, and 'Volunteers Are Shining Stars' was published
in the anthology *This Is Not Chick Lit*.

Every effort has been made to obtain the necessary permissions with
reference to copyright material, both illustrative and quoted. We apologize
for any omissions in this respect and will be pleased to make the
appropriate acknowledgements in any future edition.

A CIP catalogue record for this book
is available from the British Library.

ISBNs
9780857525383 (hb)
9780857525390 (tpb)

Typeset in 11.5/15.5pt Galliard
Printed and bound by Clays Ltd, Bungay, Suffolk

Penguin Random House is committed to a sustainable
future for our business, our readers and our planet. This book
is made from Forest Stewardship Council® certified paper.

MIX
Paper from
responsible sources
FSC® C018179

1 3 5 7 9 10 8 6 4 2

For
Susanna Daniel,
Emily Miller,
and Sheena MJ Cook—
my fellow writers and confidantes

Contents

You Think It,
I'll Say It

The Nominee

The journalist was born in 1964, which is to say she's seventeen years younger than I am. She has, starting in 1992, interviewed me several dozen times—she was at *The San Francisco Chronicle* when I met her, then moved to *The Washington Post*, and for the last eight years has been at *The New York Times*—and while we aren't friends, she reminds me of a neighbor or cousin; we didn't exactly choose each other, but we are ineluctably part of each other's lives.

What I appreciate about her is the blazing, undeniable intelligence that manifests itself in her ability, in our conversations, to recall minutiae from a transportation bill I sponsored in the Senate, or a 1994 speech I gave in Stockholm as First Lady; in her observations, appearing in her articles, of the perfect colorful detail from a state fair or pancake breakfast that I myself, sitting amidst it, missed; and in her snapping, spontaneous sense of humor. Once, at a signing ceremony for a greenhouse-gas-emissions law, when the president inadvertently referred to "hair pollution" instead of "air pollution," my eyes landed on the journalist's, and I had to look away and bite my tongue. When we spoke after the ceremony, she began by saying, "Like when you spill conditioner in the shower?" and I replied, "I was actually thinking about a certain perm I got in the mid-eighties."

The truth is that when she interviews me, I feel an alertness, a welcome kind of challenge, that's deeply satisfying. I've sometimes thought that the reason people who aren't particularly bright don't care for people who are is the hunch among the former that the latter speak to one another in code. Which we do: brain to brain, with an explanation-dispensing briskness, a shared understanding of subtext. I would never publicly admit this, least of all to her, but I believe the journalist is worthy of interviewing me in a way many kinder reporters are not.

What I care for least about the journalist is the sense of entitlement she demonstrates in small and large ways. Small: I never witness it, but according to my staff, she's a notorious pain about the logistics we've arranged for the press corps in a manner no print journalist from anywhere other than *The Times* would dare to be; she complains about which hotel room she's been assigned, or where she's sitting on the plane or bus. Large: I believe she's quite sexist and either is blind to it or, more likely, sees herself as impervious, what with her fancy education, her cynicism, and her job at the cultural nexus of our post-everything society. Over and over, year in and year out, she asks me questions she'd never ask a man running for public office, a man elected to public office, a male senator or secretary of state or presidential candidate: Who designed the pantsuit I wore to the State of the Union? How has my husband influenced my foreign-policy views, stance on minimum wage, and opinion of vegans? Do I consider my marriage to be a good one? Is the country ready for a president who's also a grandmother? And always—always—some variation on this: Why do so many voters, even ones who admire my record, have difficulty connecting with me? Why do the American people find me fundamentally unlikable?

The journalist cushions her rhetoric. She says, *Some people say . . .* or *There's concern that . . .*, as if she is a mere observer of the questions' perpetuation. She then muses over the questions, and my responses, in her articles, which have become longer, less newsy, and more leisurely and reflective as she has achieved greater professional success. Granted, it is her editors who conjure the headlines and decide upon the accompanying art: a caricature of me with eyes and mouth opened so widely I look deranged, possibly about to devour a small child; or a photograph shot close up then magnified in such a way that every line on my face is a ravine, even beneath a visibly massive quantity of powdery foundation. However, I hold the journalist accountable for steering the packaging. The words in the headlines are someone else's, but it is she who has written the original sentences resulting in a magazine cover asking (with prominent bags beneath my eyes, no less), FRONTRUNNER FATIGUE?

At this point, I expect to be burned by the journalist. No matter how friendly our encounter, how personal, even, I will at best be irritated by what she writes. Years ago, when her child was a toddler, I found myself describing the bribing-with-Skittles method of toilet-training I'd used with my own daughter; a few days later, I read the journalist's borderline defamatory article about the controversial, and unprofitable, real-estate investments my husband and I had made in the late seventies. I might be irritated while recognizing that a piece does more harm than good, or I might be irritated *and* know it will lose me votes. Nevertheless, right now, in this moment, in July 2016, in Philadelphia, Pennsylvania, deep in the bowels of the Wells Fargo Center, in the minutes before I go onstage, she—the journalist—and the photographer accompanying her are the only media in the greenroom. My husband is here, our daughter and son-in-law and grandchildren, their nanny, many members of my campaign staff—my political director and communications director and media consultant and chief strategist, a handful of policy advisors—as well as my closest friends, among them my college roommate and the woman who was the second female partner at the law firm where, in 1979, I became the first. And of course our own photographer and videographer are here, the ones who chronicle the version of the narrative I not only prefer but believe to be true. Apart from the journalist and her photographer, however, there is no press.

"Madam Secretary," the journalist says, "how are you feeling?"

"I feel great," I say. When I smile—my smile, of course, has been compared to that of a vulture and a hag, that of Lady Macbeth and Cruella de Vil and Joker from Batman—she smiles back.

"You've talked about this ad nauseam, obviously," the journalist says, "but now that it's really, officially happening—what's it like to be the first major party female nominee for president of the United States of America?"

I feel the way you felt at your high school graduation, I think. It's anticlimactic. We've been marking time, waiting for this, since April 2015, right? Or since 2007? Or perhaps since 1992 or 1969 or 1789? But I also know some specific instant tonight will seize me, will catch me off-guard in spite of myself, and I'll be struck by the enormity of the situation and probably tear up, thereby launching a thousand articles about gender and crying.

Aloud I say, "I've been preparing for this moment for my entire life. I'm confident, I'm humbled, and I'm very optimistic about the future of our country."

In 2002, when I was a senator and the journalist was at *The Washington Post*, she interviewed me in a hotel suite in San Francisco on a day on which I'd first traveled to meet the survivors of a tornado in Oklahoma and would spend the evening at a million-dollar fundraising dinner in Pacific Heights. In the suite's living room, we sat facing each other in armchairs a few feet apart; her recorder was set on a small round glass table to my left. Also in the room were my deputy chief of staff and two aides. My Secret Service agents stood outside the suite's exterior door.

The journalist has dark, short hair, and both of us were wearing pantsuits, mine navy and hers maroon (Ralph Lauren, though I'm speaking only for myself here). We'd been talking for about ten minutes, and my communications director had promised the journalist fifteen more, though I was prepared to go to twenty or even twenty-five.

"With regard to recent comments made by your colleagues on the Senate Armed Services Committee—" she began, and then her torso pitched forward and she vomited partly onto her lap, partly onto the floor, and partly onto my lap. Although it happened quickly, some impulse had told me to cup my hands together, and a portion of her vomit, which was plentiful and dark tan in color, also landed in this ad hoc receptacle. (I've always suspected she'd recently eaten curried tuna salad; I have, since 2002, never eaten curried tuna salad.) The journalist raised her head, and her expression was so stricken—a bit of vomit clung to her lips—that truly, I felt far more concerned about her than me. "Oh, my God," she said, and her face had gone pale. "I'm so sorry."

"Well, I *am* a mother," I said, "so it's not the first time. Do you think there's more coming?" Already my deputy chief of staff had sprung up and was approaching us, but her revulsion was undisguised. She's one of the most competent people I've ever worked with; she's also squeamish, and I wondered if she might be the next to unleash the contents of her stomach.

"I can't believe I—" the journalist was saying, but didn't complete the thought. Instead, again she said, "I'm so sorry."

"Are you staying in this hotel?" I asked.

The journalist nodded.

"Give her your room key," I said and gestured to my

deputy chief of staff. "She'll get a change of clothes from your suitcase and bring it back here." Unsteadily, the journalist passed off a key card—"Room 318," she called as my deputy hurried away—and, addressing my personal aide, I said, "Please bring over a glass of water." I stood, crossed the carpet, and entered the bathroom off the living room. Without closing the door, I scrubbed my hands; small brown chunks lodged in the drain. When I emerged, I asked the journalist, "Do you need to lie down?"

I could see her hesitate—it's easy enough for one workhorse to recognize another, and I knew she wanted to continue the interview—and I said, "Go into the bedroom. Put on a robe and rest on the bed, at least for a few minutes. All the linens can be changed tonight while I'm out."

Still she hesitated—behind me, I heard my two aides murmuring to each other—and I extended my hand. The journalist grasped it as she stood, and I could feel her shakiness, a literal shakiness, as we walked arm in arm into the suite's bedroom in our vomit-bedecked pantsuits; the smell was disgusting, and later that night I ended up moving to a different suite altogether. I had never been this physically close to the journalist. I escorted her to the threshold of the bathroom inside the bedroom and asked, "Shall I wait while you clean up?"

She shook her head, and when she spoke, some firmness had returned to her voice. "I don't know what came over me."

"I'll give you privacy," I said. "Take your time."

"I'm not pregnant," she said, and though I can't claim

the thought hadn't crossed my mind, it was her very ad-
amance that made me question the statement. She was
at that time recently divorced and her son was in grade
school. She didn't go on to have another baby, which, of
course, is proof of nothing.

I began to close the bathroom door and she said,
"Wait."

Our eyes met.

"I trust that this is all off the record," she said, and
even then it occurred to me that if the situation were reversed, she'd never have extended such a courtesy.

"You're in luck," I said. "Because I'm not a journalist."

"How would a female president change other countries'
perception of America?" the journalist asks in the Wells
Fargo Center's greenroom. We stand next to a long table
covered in a white cloth, beside the huge platter of sliced
pineapple and strawberries; all around us are the hum
and laughter of other conversations as well as the words
and applause from the speech currently being delivered
on the arena stage and broadcast on a TV on the greenroom wall.

I say, "I imagine many countries will be pleased that
we've caught up to a milestone they reached years ago."

"And what might your presidency mean for women?"

"If elected, I'll proudly work on behalf of all Americans."

"But it's no secret that you've always been a Rorschach
test for people in terms of where they stand on issues like

feminism and women in the workforce. Just as a symbol, you—"

I shake my head, interrupting her. "Surely you realize that no one sees herself as a symbol?"

In 1957, my friend Carol Gurski's tenth birthday party took place at her house in Park Ridge, Illinois, a block away from where my own family lived. Six of us fifth-grade girls sat at the Gurskis' dining-room table eating cake, along with Carol's younger brother; her parents stood nearby. The subject of baseball arose—I was an ardent Cubs fan, despite their terrible record that year—and I said, "Even if the White Sox are having a better season, Ernie Banks is clearly the best player on either team. If the Cubs build around him, they'll be good in time."

Carol's father was across the table, behind Carol and facing me, and he smiled unpleasantly, in a way I had never previously recognized but have observed on a daily basis ever since. He said, "You're awfully opinionated for a girl."

And, really, there are so many other words people use to express the sentiment, but I always hear the echo of Bud Gurski.

When, in a 1995 speech in Beijing, I resisted pressure from both the White House and the Chinese government to tone down my declaration that human rights are inseparable from women's rights? *You're awfully opinionated for a girl.*

When I criticized the Taliban before everyone criticized

the Taliban? *You're awfully opinionated for a girl.*

When I pushed for universal health care, a goal that turned out to be so controversial that my security detail required me for a time to wear a bulletproof vest in public? When I insisted, as secretary of state, on directly addressing with other governments the diplomatic damage wrought by the rash choices of the previous president? When I made that now-infamous crack about how I could have stayed home baking cookies and having teas? All those times, I was awfully, awfully opinionated.

During my tenure at the state department, I visited 112 countries, and much of what I did, in Pakistan and Russia, in Indonesia and Israel and Angola and El Salvador, was listen. Indeed, though I've failed at various times on various fronts, I've often thought that the bulk of my professional achievements have rested on two equally unsexy strengths: I am always willing to do my homework, and I am always willing to listen.

Also: I actually know, in a daily, granular way, what it's like to live in the White House, and the difference between thinking you know what it's like to live in the White House and living in the White House is the difference between thinking you know what it's like to be a parent and being a parent.

Yes, I get it—the typical American voter possesses no more than fleeting familiarity with my résumé while feeling that he or she has been choking on my public image and my politics for almost twenty-five years. The typical American voter doesn't wish to share a beer with me.

I have my supporters, of course, and then some. But it's a bitter pill to swallow for those who aren't in that category: that the person most qualified to be the next president is an awfully opinionated girl.

Is the journalist's sexism attributable to the age difference between us, because she always took for granted her entry into the workforce? But surely she has experienced discrimination in the newsroom, at press conferences, on campaign planes and buses? Although she seems friendly with her male colleagues, sometimes her very jocularity suggests a compensating energy.

Is it because she was just nine years old when Roe *v.* Wade was decided?

Is it because, while I grew up middle-class, she grew up rich? She's from Boston, I know, and she attended Choate and Yale.

Or is it because fundamentally, as a writer, she's a bystander instead of a participant?

We still are next to the greenroom's buffet, in this thicket of people I have known and mostly loved for many years. It's strange how much I feel and cannot say. Even stranger is how much I can say without being believed, without my words being considered anything other than hollow propaganda. The irony: I really *have* been preparing for this moment for my entire life. I actually *am* confident, humbled, and optimistic about the future of our country.

I plan to win the election in November, and I plan after that to win the reelection. I trust that Americans will become accustomed to a female president in much the way they became accustomed to a black one—in some cases enthusiastically and in others gracelessly. The thought of what will happen if I don't win, if my opponent somehow triumphs, is almost inconceivable, less for me personally than for our country. I am not exaggerating when I say it could be catastrophic; fortunately, I also don't believe it will occur.

Thus, it will likely be January 2025 when my presidency concludes. I will be seventy-seven years old, and the journalist sixty-one; we'll have known each other for more than three decades. And undoubtedly, before I return after so long to private life (Will I ever return to private life? Presumably not really, but such things are relative, and I might feel as if I have), the journalist and I will have one final encounter: my exit interview.

How delicious it will be to stop trying to *convince* people! To stop pretending that I don't hear the criticism, or that I don't care about it—there are, of course, ways in which I really don't hear it and really don't care about it, but neither can be entirely true so long as a heart still beats inside my chest. But it will be only after my long stretch in the public eye has concluded, after all my bids for quantifiable and unquantifiable approval, that I can be honest with the journalist and by extension with the American people.

The journalist will end my exit interview in the way she ends all interviews, which is by saying, "Is there anything I should be asking you that I'm not?"

I cannot lie; more than once I've been tempted to say, *Do you remember when I caught your curried-tuna vomit in my hands? Because I do.* But the truth is that I had forgiven her even before she finished throwing up; that, at least, was out of her control. So, no. Such a question would be a waste.

Instead—I'll be casual, as if it's an afterthought—I'll say this: "You've mentioned many times over the years that you find me unlikable. How do you think I find *you*?"

Gender Studies

Nell and Henry always said that they would wait until marriage was legal for everyone in America, and now this is the case—it's August 2015—but earlier in the week Henry eloped with his graduate student Bridget. Bridget is twenty-three, moderately but not dramatically attractive (one of the few nonstereotypical aspects of the situation, Nell thinks, is Bridget's lack of dramatic attractiveness), and Henry and Bridget had been dating for six months. They began having an affair last winter, when Henry and Nell were still together; then in April, Henry moved out of the house he and Nell own and into Bridget's apartment. Nell and Henry had been a couple for eleven years.

In the shuttle between the Kansas City airport and the hotel where Nell's weekend meetings will occur—the shuttle is a van, and she is its only passenger—a radio host and a guest are discussing the presidential candidacy of Donald Trump. The driver catches Nell's eye in the rearview mirror and says, "He's not afraid to speak his mind, huh? You gotta give him that."

Nell makes a nonverbal sound to acknowledge that, in the most literal sense, she heard the comment.

The driver says, "I never voted before, but, he makes it all the way, maybe I will. A tough businessman like that could go kick some butts in Washington."

There was a time, up to and including the recent past, when Nell would have said something calm but repudiating in response, something professorial, or at least intended as such. Perhaps: *What is it about Trump's business record that you find most persuasive?* But now she thinks, You're a moron. All she says is "Interesting," then she looks out the window, at the humidly overcast sky and the prairies behind ranch-style wooden fencing. Though she lives in Wisconsin, not so many states away, she has never been to Kansas City, or even to Missouri.

"I'm not a Republican," the driver says. "But I'm not a Democrat, either, that's for sure. You wouldn't *never* catch me voting for Shrillary." He shudders, or mock-shudders. "If I was Bill, I'd cheat on her, too."

The driver appears to be in his early twenties, fifteen or so years younger than Nell, with narrow shoulders on a tall frame over which he wears a shiny orange polo shirt; the van is also orange, and an orange ballpoint pen is set behind his right ear. He has nearly black hair that is combed back and looks wet, and the skin on his face is pale white and pockmarked. In the rearview mirror, he and Nell make eye contact again, and he says, "I'm not sexist."

Nell says nothing.

"You married?" he asks.

"No," she says.

"Boyfriend?"

"No," she says again, then immediately regrets it—he gave her two chances, and she failed to take either.

"Me, I'm divorced," he says. "Never getting wrapped up in that again. But I've got a four-year-old, Lisette. Total daddy's girl. You have kids?"

"No." This she has no desire to lie about.

Will he scold her? He doesn't. Instead, he asks, "You a lawyer?"

She actually smiles. "You mean like Hillary? No. I'm a professor."

"A professor of what?"

"English." Now she *is* lying. She is a professor of gender and women's studies, but outside academia it's often easier not to get into it.

She pulls her phone from the jacket she's wearing because of how cold the air-conditioning is and says, in a brisk tone, "I need to send an email." Instead, she checks to see how much longer it will take to get to the hotel— twenty-two minutes, apparently. The interruption works, and he doesn't try to talk to her again until they're downtown, off the highway. In the meantime, via Facebook, she accidentally discovers that Henry and Bridget, who got married two days ago in New Orleans (why New Orleans? Nell has no idea), had a late breakfast of beignets this morning and, as of an hour ago, were strolling around the French Quarter.

"How long you in K.C.?" the driver asks as he stops the van beneath the hotel's porte cochere. The driveway is busy with other cars coming and going and valets and bellhops sweating in maroon uniforms near automatic glass doors.

"Until Sunday," Nell says.

"Business or pleasure?"

It's the midyear planning meeting for the governing board of the national association of which Nell is the most recent past president, all of which sounds so boring that she is perversely tempted to describe it to him. But she simply says, "Business."

"You have free time, you should check out our barbecue," the guy says. "Best ribs in town are at Winslow's. You're not a vegetarian, are you?"

She and Henry were both vegetarians when they met, which was in graduate school; he was getting a PhD in political science. Then, about five years ago, by coincidence, Henry went to a restaurant where Nell was having lunch with a friend. Nell was eating a BLT. Neither she nor Henry said anything until that night at home, when she asked, "Did you notice what was on my plate today?"

"Actually," Henry said, "I've been eating meat, too."

Nell was stunned. Not upset but truly shocked. She said, "Since when?"

"A year?" Henry looked sheepish as he added, "It's just so satisfying."

They laughed, and they started making steak for dinner, or sausage, although, because of the kind of people they were (insufferable people, Nell thinks now), it had to be grass-fed or free-range or organic. And not too frequent.

All of which is to say that many times since she learned of Henry's affair she has wondered not only if she should have known but even if she is at fault for not cheating on him. Was there an unspoken pact that she failed to discern? And, either way, hadn't she been warned? An admiring twenty-three-year-old graduate student was, presumably, just so satisfying! Plus, Bridget and Henry had become involved at a time when Nell and Henry could go months without sex. They still got along well enough, but if they had ever felt passion or excitement—and truly, in retrospect, she can't remember if they did—they didn't anymore. Actually, what she remembers from their courtship is dinners at a not very good Mexican restaurant near campus, during which she could tell that he was trying to seem smart to her in exactly the way that she was trying to seem smart to him. Maybe for them that *was* passion? Simultaneously, she is furious at him—she feels the standard humiliation and betrayal—and she also feels an unexpected sympathy, which she has been careful not to express to him or to her friends. Their deliberately childless life, their cat, Converse (named not for the shoe but for the political scientist), their free-range beef and nights and weekends of reading and grading and high-quality television series—it was fine and a little horrible. She gets it.

To the driver, she says, "I'm not a vegetarian."

He turns off the van's engine. Although she paid online, in advance, for the ride, an engraved plastic sign above the rearview mirror reads, TIPS NOT REQUIRED BUT APPRECIATED. As he climbs out of the front seat to retrieve her suitcase from the rear of the van, she sees that all she has in her wallet is twenties. If it weren't for his political commentary, she would give him one—her general stance is that if she can pay three hundred dollars for a pair of shoes or $11.99 a pound for Thai broccoli salad from the co-op, she can overtip hourly wage workers—but now she hesitates. She'll ask for ten back, she decides.

She joins the driver behind the van, just as a town car goes by. When she passes him a twenty, she observes him registering the denomination and possibly developing some parting fondness for her. Which means that she can't bring herself to ask for ten back, so instead she says, "There's no way Donald Trump will be the Republican nominee for president."

She wonders if he'll say something like "Fuck you, lady," but he gives no such gratification. He says, seeming concerned, "Hey, I didn't mean offense." From a pocket in his pants he takes a white business card with an orange stripe and the shuttle logo on the front. He adds, "I'm not driving Sunday, but, you need anything while you're here, just call me." Then he kneels, takes the ballpoint pen from behind his ear, and uses her black-wheeled suitcase, which is upright on the ground between them, as a desk. He writes LUKE in capital letters and a ten-digit number underneath. (Years ago, Henry had tied a checked red-and-white ribbon, from a Christmas gift his mother had sent them, to the suitcase's handle.) The driver holds the business card up to her.

For what earthly reason would she call him? But the unsettling part is that, with him kneeling, it happens that his face is weirdly close to the zipper of her pants—he didn't do this on purpose, she doesn't think, but his face is maybe three inches away—so how could the idea of him performing oral sex on her *not* flit across her mind? In a clipped voice, she says, "Thanks for the ride."

With CNN on in the background, Nell hangs her shirts and pants in the hotel room closet and carries her Dopp kit into the bathroom. The members of the governing board will meet in the lobby at six and take taxis to a restaurant a mile away. Nell is moving the things she won't need at dinner out of her purse and setting them on top of the bureau—a water bottle, a manila folder containing the notes for a paper she's in the revise-and-resubmit stage with—when she notices that her driver's license isn't in the front slot of her wallet, behind the clear plastic window. Did she not put it back after going through security in the Madison airport? She isn't particularly worried until she has searched her entire purse twice, and then she is worried. She also doesn't find the license in the pockets of her pants or her jacket, and it wouldn't be in her suitcase. She pictures her license sitting by itself in one of those small, round gray containers at the end of the X-ray belt—the head shot from 2010, taken soon after she got reddish highlights, the numbers specifying her date of birth and height and weight and address. But she didn't set it in any such container. She probably dropped it on the carpet while walking to her gate, or it fell out of her bag or her pocket on the plane.

Can you board a plane in the United States, in 2015, without an ID? If you're a white woman, no doubt your chances are higher than anyone else's. According to the Internet, she should arrive at the airport early and plan to show other forms of ID, some of which she has (a work badge, a gym ID, a business card) and some of which she doesn't (a utility bill, a check, a marriage license). She calls the airline, which feels like a futile kind of due diligence. The next call she makes is to the van driver—thank goodness for the twenty-dollar tip—who answers the phone by saying, in a professional tone, "This is Luke."

"This is the person who was your passenger to the Garden Center Hotel," Nell says. "You dropped me off about forty-five minutes ago."

"Hey there." Immediately, Luke sounds warmer.

Trying to match his warmth, she says, "I might have left my driver's license in your van. Can you check for me? My name is Eleanor Davies."

"I'm driving now, but I'll look after this drop-off, no problem."

Impulsively, Nell says, "If you find it, I'll pay you." Should she specify an amount? Another twenty? Fifty?

"Well, it's here or it's not," Luke says. "I'll call you back."

"I was sitting in the first row, behind you," Nell says, and when Luke speaks again, he seems amused.

He says, "Yeah, I remember."

He hasn't called by the time she has to go to dinner. She calls him again before leaving her room, but the call goes to voicemail. The dinner, attended by nine people, including Nell, is more fun than she expected—they spend a good chunk of it discussing a gender-studies department in California that's imploding, plus they drink six bottles of wine—and the group decides to walk back to the hotel. In her room, Nell realizes that, forty-two minutes ago, she received a call from Luke, and then a text. "Hey call me," the text reads.

"You at the hotel now?" he says when she calls, and when she confirms that she is, he says, "My shift just ended, so I can be there in fifteen."

"Wow, thank you so much," Nell says. "I really appreciate this." He will text when he arrives, they agree, and she'll go outside.

Except that when she reaches the lobby, he's standing inside it, near the glass doors. He's not wearing the shiny orange polo shirt; he has on dark gray jeans and a black, hooded, sleeveless shirt. His biceps are stringily well-defined; also, the shirt makes her cringe. She has decided to give him forty dollars, which she's folded in half and is holding out even before they speak. He waves away the money and says, "Buy me a drink and we'll call it even."

"Buy you a drink?" she repeats. If she were sober, she'd definitely make an excuse.

With his chin, Luke gestures across the lobby toward the hotel bar, from which come boisterous conversations and the notes of a live saxophone player. "One Jack and Coke," he says. "You ask me, you're getting a bargain."

Having a drink in the hotel bar with Luke the Shuttle Driver is almost enjoyable, because it's like an anthropological experience. Beyond her wish to get her license back, she feels no fondness for the person sitting across the table, but the structure of his life, the path that brought him from birth to this moment, is interesting in the way that anyone's is. He's twenty-seven, older than she guessed, born in Wichita, the second of two brothers. His parents split up before his second birthday; he's met his father a handful of times and doesn't like him.

He'll never disappear from his daughter's life the way that his father disappeared from his. He and his mom and his brother moved to Kansas City when he was in fifth grade—her parents are from here—and he played baseball in junior high and high school and hoped for a scholarship to Truman State (a scout even came to one of his games), but senior year he tore his UCL. After that, he did a semester at UMKC, but the classes were boring and not worth the money. ("No offense," he says, as if Nell, by virtue of being a professor, had a hand in running them.) He met his ex-wife, Shelley, in high school, but the funny thing is that he didn't like her that much then, so he should have known. He thinks she just wanted a kid. They were married for two years, and now she's dating someone else from their high school class, and Luke thinks better that guy than him. Luke and his buddy Tim want to start their own shuttle service, definitely in the next eighteen months; the manager of the one he's working for now is a dick.

Eliciting this information isn't difficult. The one question he asks her is how many years she had to go to school to become a professor. She says, "How many after high school or how many total?"

"After high school," he says, and she says, "Nine."

Without consulting her, he orders them a second round, and after finishing it Nell is the drunkest she's been since she was a bridesmaid in her friend Anna's wedding, in 2003; she's wall-shiftingly drunk. She says, "Okay, give me my license now."

Luke grins. "How 'bout I walk you to your room? Be a gentleman and all."

"That's subtle," she says. Does he know what *subtle*

means? (It's not that she's unaware that she's an elitist asshole. She's aware! She's just powerless not to be one. Also, seriously, does he know what *subtle* means?) She says, "Is hitting on passengers a thing with you, or should I feel special?"

"What makes you think I'm hitting on you?" But he's still grinning, and it's the first thing he's said that a man she'd want to go out with would say. (How will she ever, in real life, meet a man she wants to go out with who wants to go out with her? Should she join Match? Tinder? Will her students find her there?) Then Luke says, "Just kidding, I'm totally hitting on you," and it's double the exact right thing to say—he has a sense of humor *and* he's complimenting her.

She says, "If you give me my license, you can walk me to my room."

"Let me walk you to your room, and I'll give you your license."

Is this how the heroines of romance novels feel? They have, in air quotes, no choice but to submit; they are absolved of responsibility by extenuating circumstances. (Semi-relatedly, Nell was once the first author on a paper titled "Booty Call: Norms of Restricted and Unrestricted Sociosexuality in Hookup Culture," a paper that, when she last checked Google Scholar, which was yesterday, had been cited thirty-one times.)

Nell charges the drinks to her room, and in the elevator up to the seventh floor he is standing behind her, and presses his face between her neck and shoulder and it feels really good; when they are configured like this, it's difficult to remember that she's not attracted to him. Inside her room—the pretense that he is merely walking her to the door has apparently dissolved—they make out for a while by the bathroom. (It's weird, but not bad-weird, to be kissing a man other than Henry. She has not done so for eleven years.) Then they're horizontal on the king-sized bed, on top of the white down comforter. They roll over a few times, but mostly she's under him. Eventually, he unbuttons and removes her blouse, then her bra, then pulls off his ridiculous hooded shirt. (Probably, if she were less drunk, she'd turn out the light on the nightstand.) He's taller and thinner than Henry, and he uses his hands in a less habitually proficient but perhaps more natively adept way. He smells like some very fake, very male kind of body wash or deodorant. Intermittently, she thinks of how amused her friend Lisa, who's an economics professor, will be when she texts her to say that she had a one-night stand with the shuttle driver. Though, for it to count as a one-night stand, is penetration required? *Will* penetration occur? Maybe, if he has a condom.

He's assiduously licking her left nipple, then her right one, then kissing down her sternum, though he stops above her navel and starts to come back up. She says, "Keep going," and when he raises his head to look at her, she says, "You're allowed to go down on me." This is not a thing she ever said to Henry. Although he did it—not often but occasionally, in years past—neither of them treated it like a privilege she was bestowing.

Luke pulls down her pants and her underwear at the same time. He has to stand to get them over her ankles. From above her, he says, "Wow, you haven't shaved lately, huh? Not a fan of the Brazilian?"

Which might stop her cold if he were a person whose

opinion she cared about, a person she'd ever see again. She knows from her students that being mostly or completely hairless is the norm now, unremarkable even among those who consider themselves ardent feminists, and it occurs to her that she may well be the oldest woman Luke has ever hooked up with.

The funny, awful part is that she *did* shave recently—she shaved her so-called bikini line this morning in the shower, because she had seen online that the hotel has a pool and had packed her bathing suit, which in fact is not a bikini. Lightly, she says to Luke, "You're very chivalrous."

Their eyes meet—she's perhaps 3 percent less hammered than she was in the lobby, though still hammered enough not to worry about her drunkenness wearing off anytime soon—and at first he says nothing. Then, so seriously that his words almost incite in her a genuine emotion, he says, "You're pretty."

With her cooperation, he tugs her body toward the foot of the bed, so that her legs are dangling off it, then he kneels on the floor and begins his ministrations. (Being eaten out by the shuttle driver! While naked! With the lights on! In Kansas City! Lisa is going to find this hilarious.) Pretty soon, Nell stops thinking of Lisa. Eventually, wondrously, there is the surge, then the cascade. Though she doesn't do it, it crosses her mind to say "I love you" to Luke. That is, in such a situation she can understand why a person would.

He is next to her on the bed again—he's naked, too, though she doesn't recall when he removed the rest of his clothes—and she closes her eyes as she reaches for his erection and starts moving her hand. In spite of the impulse to declare her love, she's still not crazy about the sight of him. She says, "I'll give you a blow job, but I want my license first. For real."

He doesn't respond, and she stops moving her hand. She says, "Just get it and put it on the bedside table. Then we can quit discussing this."

In a small voice, he says, "I don't have it."

Her eyes flap open. "Seriously?"

"I checked the van, but it wasn't there."

"Are you kidding me?" She sits up. "Then what the fuck are you doing here?"

He says nothing, and she says, "You lied to me."

He shrugs. "I wish I had it."

"Are you planning to, like, sell it?" Who do people sell licenses to? she wonders. Underage kids? Identity thieves?

"I told you, I don't have it."

"Well, it's not like you have any credibility at this point."

After a beat, he says, "Or maybe you didn't really lose it."

"What's that supposed to mean?"

She will reflect on this moment later, will reflect on it extensively, and one of the conclusions she'll come to is that, with more self-possession, he could have recalibrated the mood. He could have done a variation on the thing he did in the bar, when he teased her for assuming he was hitting on her and then admitted he was hitting on her. If he had been more confident, that is, or presumptuous, even—if he'd jokingly pointed out her glaring and abundant complicity. But her life has probably given her far more practice at presumption than his has given him. And, in reality, he looks scared of her. His looking scared makes her feel like a scary woman, and the feeling is both repugnant and pleasurable.

Quietly, he says, "I swear I don't have it."

"You should leave," she says, then adds, "Now."

Again when they look at each other, she is close to puncturing the theatrics of her own anger—certainly she is not oblivious of the nonequitability of their encounter ending at this moment—but she hasn't yet selected the words she'll use to cause the puncture. As drunk as she is, the words are hard to find.

"I thought we were having fun." His tone is a little pathetic and also a little accusing. "*You* had fun." It's his stating what she has already acknowledged to herself, what she was considering acknowledging to him, that definitively tips the scales the wrong way.

"Get out," she says.

In her peripheral vision, as she looks at her bare legs, she can see him stand and dress. Her heart is beating rapidly. Clothed, he folds his arms. If he'd reached for her shoulder . . . If he'd sat back down next to her . . .

"Eleanor," he says, and this is the first and only time he uses her name, which of course is her real name, though not one that anybody who knows her calls her by. "I wasn't trying to trick you. I just wanted to hang out."

She says nothing, and after a minute he walks to the door and leaves.

Her headache lasts until midafternoon on Saturday, through the budget meeting, the meeting about the newly proposed journal, the discussion of where to hold future conferences after the ones that are scheduled for

2016 and 2017. She suspects that some of her colleagues are hungover, too, and she'd likely be hungover, anyway, without the additional drinks she had with Luke, so it's almost as if the Luke interlude didn't occur—as if it were a brief and intensely enjoyable dream that took a dreadful turn. And yet, after she wakes from a pre-dinner nap, the meetings are a blur and the time with Luke is painfully vivid.

Nell rises from bed and splashes cold water on her face. She wants days and weeks to have passed, so that she can revert to being her boring self, her wronged-by-her-partner, high-road self; she wants to build up the capital, if only in her own mind, of not being cruel. She no longer thinks she'll tell Lisa anything.

Which means that when, while dressing to meet her colleagues for dinner, she finds her driver's license in the left pocket of her jacket, the discovery only amplifies her distress. The lining of the jacket's left pocket is ripped, which she knew about, because a dime has been slipping around inside it since last spring. But she hadn't realized that the hole was large enough for a license to pass through.

When she was a sophomore in high school, the father of a kind and popular classmate died of cancer. Nell didn't know the boy well, and she wasn't sure if it was appropriate to write him a condolence note. He came back to school after a week, at which point she hadn't written one. It seemed like perhaps it was too late. But a few days later, she wondered, *Had* it been too late? Weeks later, was it too late? Months? She occasionally still recalls this boy, now a man who is, like her, nearly forty, and she wishes she had expressed compassion.

This is how she will feel about Luke. She could have summoned him back on Friday night. She could have called him on Saturday, after finding the license. She could have texted him on Sunday, or when she returned to Madison. However, though she thinks of him regularly—she thinks of him especially during the Republican debates, then during the primaries, the caucuses, the convention, and the election (the election!)—she never initiates contact. She does join Match, she goes to a salon and gets fully waxed, she starts dating an architect she didn't meet on Match, who is eight years older than her, pro women's pubic hair, and appalled by how readily a gender-studies professor will capitulate to arbitrary standards of female beauty. Nell finds his view to be a relief personally, but intellectually a facile and unendearing failure of imagination.

Sometimes, when she's half asleep, she remembers Luke saying, "You're pretty," how serious and sincere his voice was. She remembers when his face was between her legs, and she feels shame and desire. But by daylight it's hard not to mock her own overblown emotions. He didn't have anything to do with her losing the license, no, but it's his fault that she thought he did. Besides, he was a Trump supporter.

The World Has Many Butterflies

Julie and Graham had known each other for eight years before they ever played I'll Think It, You Say It, then they played I'll Think It, You Say It for a year before Julie decided—decided, realized, idiotically fabricated the belief that—she was in love with Graham. Graham worked at the same investment banking firm in Houston as Julie's husband. Also, their respective kids all attended the same private school, which meant Julie and Keith saw Graham and his wife, Gayle, regularly, in a way that (for almost a decade!) had barely registered with Julie. They showed up at the same soccer games and school fundraisers and Christmas parties and dinner parties. They greeted one another in a friendly fashion, and—in retrospect, Julie went over it repeatedly, that innocent earlier era before she became obsessed—she thought of Graham as slightly more appealing than most men, but neither fascinating nor smolderingly handsome. Even later, Julie considered Graham and Keith comparably attractive, if your thing was preppy middle-aged men, which hers apparently was. But neither of them was, like, *hot*. Nevertheless, for a stretch of several months, whenever Julie had sex with her husband, she pretended he was Graham.

It was at Bret and Tracy Hutchinson's twentieth anniversary party, at River Oaks Country Club, that Graham appeared beside Julie and said, for the first time, "I'll think it, you say it." Julie was standing alone, momentarily, because the babysitter had texted to ask if her youngest child was allowed to go to sleep with the light on in his room. Graham nodded his head once, toward an unofficial receiving line that had formed around the party's hosts.

"Well, for starters," Julie said, "I'm surprised they decided to throw this party because I was always under the impression Bret and Tracy kind of hate each other." She glanced at Graham before adding, "I assume they're celebrating, what, a total of three happy years together?"

Graham raised his eyebrows. "I'd have estimated one, but, sure, let's round up."

"And even though they're both tedious, they're tedious in such distinctive ways," Julie said. "With him, it's like, all roads eventually lead to a disquisition on the pleasures of hunting white-tailed deer. But apart from being bloodthirsty, he's really gentle and has such good manners. Whereas with her, all roads lead to her gifted children, and she's so aggressive and braggy. Literally, she's probably told me twelve times that Mr. Vaughn said Fritz is the most talented math student he's ever had." Julie took a sip of her champagne before adding, "To be fair, Tracy does look great tonight. Her Spanx must be killing her, but she looks great."

"What are Spanx?" Graham asked.

"Seriously? They're 'shapewear.' " Julie made air quotes. "They smooth out your womanly lumps and bumps."

"And here I thought womanly lumps and bumps were one of life's great gifts," Graham said.

"Depending on the location." When Julie and Graham's eyes met, she said, "Who else?"

Graham nodded toward another guest and said, "Anne Pyland."

"Anne is an interesting case, because every other time I interact with her, I either get a kick out of her or I can't stand her. So in the end, even though she's better *and* worse than most people, she's average. When she's in a bad mood, she doesn't hide it, and I'm not sure if I'm jealous or appalled."

Again, Graham nodded once. "Rob Greffkamp."

"He's wondering how many drinks he needs to consume before he can forget his moral ambivalence about working for Halliburton." From across the room, Rob Greffkamp let loose with boisterous laughter, and Julie added, "And he's optimistic that he's at least halfway there."

"Sherry Chessel."

"Bad news," Julie said. "I really like Sherry. I have nothing critical to say."

Graham gave her a dubious look. "Surely if you put your mind to it?"

"Graham, she's the director of an organization that finds families for foster kids. Plus, she has a sense of humor."

"Fair enough. Doug Green."

"For Doug, we go to the multiple choice format: (A) super-snobby and aloof, (B) intensely awkward, or (C) on the spectrum." Julie looked at Graham. "Don't tell me you haven't considered all those possibilities."

"A combination of A and B," Graham said. "Is that permitted?"

"It is," Julie said, "although it's a cop-out."

"Jennifer Reilly."

"Well, she can't stand Anne, so it's funny they're talking to each other right now," Julie said. "Were you guys at the school auction last spring?"

Graham nodded.

"I think Jennifer had just had a lot of the punch, but Anne spread rumors that she'd snorted coke."

"Man," Graham said. "You're good."

"By which I assume you mean I'm a huge bitch who usually manages to keep her bitchiness concealed?"

Was Julie a huge bitch who usually managed to keep her bitchiness concealed? She truly didn't know. In the eight years she and Keith had lived in Houston, she had never talked like this to anyone. She was simultaneously shocked by the conversation, shocked to be having it with a man, shocked by its effortlessness, and not surprised at all; it was as if she'd been waiting to be recognized, as if she'd never sung in public, then someone had handed her a microphone and she'd opened her mouth and released a full-throated vibrato. Except that her only audience was Graham, a familiar semi-stranger, which made the game a secret, which was the most fun part of all. Neither on that day nor in the future did they ever discuss the game's rules, yet clearly they both agreed what they were. Julie considered this complicity amazing, though she wondered if her bar for amazing was low.

She did have friends, and they did gossip about people,

but the way they gossiped felt superficial, imprecise, and gratuitously mean; talking to Graham felt sincere and only incidentally mean. Also, there was a physical sensation Julie often had near the end of parties or kids' soccer games, what she thought of as tired face—she'd exerted herself, received little in return, and now wished to be alone, or at least to be in her car, with only children, and preferably only ones to whom she was related—and this sensation seemed, after she and Graham started playing I'll Think It, You Say It, like nothing but boredom. Was it possible she had been bored for the entire time she and Keith had lived in Houston? For her entire adulthood? Because, alarmingly, I'll Think It, You Say It left her as cheerful and energized as a Zumba class.

Julie and Keith had met in graduate school—he was getting an MBA, she a degree in speech and language pathology—and they'd married while living in Chicago, which was where their two daughters were born. Their son was born after they moved to Houston for Keith's job, and at first it amused Julie and Keith that they'd spawned a Texan. There were things about the white, moneyed version of Houston that Julie didn't love and, even more, that she didn't love herself for not resisting.

Already, by the time they'd moved, she'd stopped working. At the school where they enrolled the children, lots of mothers did drop-off in expensive exercise wear that flattered their svelte figures, then did pickup in the same expensive exercise wear; whether they had exercised in the intervening hours wasn't clear. Their hair was stylishly cut and dyed, and some of them underwent cosmetic surgery procedures, procedures other than Botox, with which Julie had previously been unfamiliar: hyaluronic-acid lip filling and laser resurfacing and abdominoplasties. In the air she breathed, there was much football, hunting, and Christianity, though Houston was big and diverse enough that she could sneak away for a solo lunch at a Sri Lankan restaurant, or do phone banking for a pro-choice congressional candidate in a tight race.

In her younger years, when single, Julie had thought of herself as a big-boobed, curly-haired, high-spirited Jewish girl, and she had heard rumors of men who appreciated these qualities, but she had not encountered them personally; perhaps, she thought, they clustered on the coasts. By the time she and Graham started playing I'll Think It, You Say It, she was no longer big-boobed (the one procedure she underwent, after nursing three kids, was a breast reduction and lift), not curly-haired (she had regular blowouts and tried to believe that the formaldehyde in the straightening lotion was offset by purchasing almost exclusively organic produce), and barely Jewish (Keith was Episcopal, and while Julie's attendance at temple was spotty, they always celebrated Christmas). Also, she wasn't really that high-spirited anymore, though neither was she unhappy. Keith worked long hours but made a lot of money, and he was rarely grumpy, often boyishly upbeat, and generally appreciative of the ways in which she exerted herself on behalf of their household. When initiating sex in bed at night, he'd say in a warm tone, "Is your vagina open for business?" Which, admittedly, caused her to cringe but was the result of a time years before when she'd had a UTI and told him her vagina was closed, so she was at least partly to blame.

At the Hutchinsons' anniversary party, Graham said to her, "I *hope* you're a huge bitch who usually manages to keep her bitchiness concealed. Otherwise, what's the point?"

Julie laughed. It wasn't that talking to Graham had made her feel lovestruck, not remotely, not then. It was more that it had made her feel big-boobed, curly-haired, high-spirited, and Jewish. Even if it was only by that point symbolic rather than literal, it had made her feel like herself.

For many months—for the next year—Julie was fine. She'd look for Graham at parties or on the sidelines of athletic fields, but casually, not frantically, and sometimes they'd speak for twenty minutes and sometimes just for three or four. They never played the game in front of other people, including either of their spouses, but in some ways the suspension of the game created an even more pleasing undercurrent than actually playing it.

Once, at pickup after a seventh birthday party attended by both of their youngest children—Julie's son, Lucas, was in the same grade as Graham's daughter Macy—Graham sidled up to her and said, "I'll think it, you say it?"

Julie smiled but shook her head. "There's no time." The party had featured a bounce house on the host family's enormous front lawn, and already the children's shoes were back on and goody bags were being distributed.

"Oh, please," Graham said. "There's always time for a quickie."

"In that case," Julie said, and she began quietly laying into the birthday boy's parents, evangelicals who owned a national chain of highly successful fast casual restaurants. But Graham's expression of possible amusement or skepticism made her pause, and she said, "Although maybe you disagree with me?"

"No, no," Graham said quickly. "Unless I tell you otherwise, you should assume we're in total agreement."

There was something strange about the happiness this comment induced in Julie, and it took her until later in the day, long after her departure from the party, to figure out what it was: Despite the location of its origins, it had been a happiness wholly unattached to her children; it had been a grown-up happiness.

On the October night that Keith came home from work and mentioned that Graham and Gayle had separated and were getting a divorce—he seemed to consider the news sad but unremarkable, and was surprised Julie didn't already know—Julie's agitation was so immediate, extreme, and difficult to conceal from Keith that surely something untoward had been percolating in her all along. The upending of her equilibrium—it was disastrous and thrilling. She truly had not known it was still possible to feel this kind of physical excitement.

In bed that night, she lay awake hour after hour and considered the situation from every angle, vacillating between lucidity and craziness. She and Graham were, obviously, in love with each other. He had left Gayle for her. (Obviously, he had not left Gayle for her.) They needed to be extremely careful, to treat their attraction like a pipe bomb. Or maybe life was short and they owed it to themselves to take advantage of every precious moment, possibly by fucking in a supply closet at River Oaks Country Club.

They would never acknowledge it.

She would say something the next time she saw him.

After three A.M., Julie fell asleep, and she woke before five, resolute. The next time she saw Graham, she'd say nothing out of the ordinary and simply use the opportunity to acquire data.

At no point had she previously considered cheating on Keith; indeed, she'd felt slightly terrified by the divorces of other couples, as if they were a communicable disease. But apparently life contained surprises. Second acts! She was forty-four.

Oddly, Julie couldn't remember whether she and Graham were in the habit of embracing when they greeted each other. Usually not, she concluded, or maybe not during the day but sometimes at adult events, at night, when alcohol was or would be involved.

Gayle came without him to a black-tie fundraiser for cancer research, after Julie had taken particular care with her appearance in anticipation of seeing him there. (Uncomfortably, Julie actually liked Gayle. She was pretty and kind, a petite woman with a brunette bob, and she'd always struck Julie, though maybe this was erroneous, as someone who found being a mother and a volunteer gratifying and sufficient.)

Julie finally saw Graham at a high school girls' basketball game on a Saturday afternoon; Julie's oldest and

Graham's middle child were a year apart but on the same team. Julie climbed up the bleachers and sat with him, her heart hammering. He was alone, and she'd come with Lucas, who was scampering around the basketball court's periphery. Julie frowned and said, "I'm sorry about you and Gayle," and then she had difficulty listening to him because she was thinking about what she'd say next, what it might reveal about her, and whether he'd find it funny. Also, when was the part when they'd have sex?

He raised his eyebrows in a rueful way and said, "Divorce is the worst, Julie. The very, very worst. But Gayle's and mine has been a long time coming."

"Everything is so complicated, isn't it?" Julie said.

Graham turned his head, and his expression was odd—it was both mournful and a little arch. He said, "Thank you for existing with me in this cosmos."

It was early November, and she decided to maintain the status quo until January because she didn't want to actively be cheating on Keith for what was probably the last Christmas that their youngest child would believe in Santa; she wanted to enjoy the holidays with a heart that was, if not uncorrupted, then only passively corrupt. She'd move forward with Graham in the new year.

For the lunch where Julie was planning to confess her love, her criteria for the restaurant had been a place where (1) it wouldn't be weird to order a glass of wine and (2) they were unlikely to run into people they knew. She decided on the restaurant inside the Four Seasons, which soon seemed humiliating—*of course* she'd considered the convenience of adjourning to a room, though she was planning on Graham being the one to suggest the adjournment. She'd contacted Graham by email, the first email she'd ever sent him, and she'd guessed correctly at his work email address based on Keith's. *I wonder if you're free to have lunch next week,* she'd written, and he'd written back, *Hi Julie! I can't do next week, but I can do Tues or Fri of the week after.*

Graham arrived ten minutes late, seeming preoccupied in exactly the way Keith was when his attention got pulled from office matters during the day; if anything, Graham seemed less chipper than Keith would under such circumstances. Later she guessed that Graham had imagined she was about to ask him to, say, join the host committee for the annual gala of the homeless shelter on whose board Julie served. Or possibly he'd thought she was hoping to fix him up with a single woman she knew; no doubt this had begun happening, which was part of why Julie couldn't delay. At the time, though, Julie had thought that Graham knew, more or less, why she'd invited him to lunch, and even afterward she wasn't convinced she'd been wrong.

By the time he sat, she'd already consumed most of her glass of white wine. They discussed Graham's older son's college applications (his first choice was Duke, though Graham considered this unrealistic). After they'd placed their orders with the waiter, Graham leaned in and said, "What's up?"

He was wearing a gray suit, a light blue shirt, and a dark blue tie with red stripes, and he was painfully attractive to her. He had hazel eyes with crow's-feet around them, a strong jaw, and completely gray hair, though he was only a year older than Julie.

She said, "This is hard to say—" and paused and looked at him, and there was nothing encouraging in his expression. If anything, a kind of cloudiness had overtaken his face. So should she have stopped? Or was some ritual degradation necessary, and if she hadn't gone through with it in the moment, she'd just have had to enact it in the future? She said, "Lately, I've been having trouble sleeping. Ever since I heard that you and Gayle had separated—I keep picturing you and me—"

Six months after Lucas was born, Julie had been shopping alone at a boutique, examining a tunic on a hanger, when a fellow shopper, a chic woman about thirty years her senior, had said, "That looks comfy!" The woman had lightly patted her own midsection and added with a smile, "Not much longer for you, I'm guessing?" That the woman assumed she was pregnant wasn't as horrifying to Julie as the prospect of what they'd both do when Julie had to reveal she wasn't. She was flustered enough that it didn't occur to her that she could simply pretend the woman was correct, and her focus was on preventing the woman from explicitly articulating her assumption. Julie extended one arm, palm out, as if to physically stop the next words. She said, overly warmly and loudly, "They sell so much great stuff here, don't they?" Then she hastily rehung the tunic and bolted from the store.

Graham did a variation on this. He said, interrupting her, "Julie—no—I don't think—" They both were silent for a few confusing but probably terrible seconds. "I don't—" Graham said, then paused again, then said,

"You and Keith seem like you have a good marriage, and God knows how rare those are. That's not something to trifle with."

She shouldn't have offered a counterargument, right? But she said, "I think about you all the time. I feel a way I haven't felt since I was a teenager."

"Keith is my co-worker, Julie. And with our kids and school—" They made excruciating eye contact, and Graham said, "It's a nonstarter."

"Do you not feel like we connect in some unusual way?"

He shrugged. "You're fun to talk to. But that doesn't necessarily mean anything beyond itself."

Although her internal organs had begun to liquefy and collapse, it seemed important to conceal this from him.

"So," he said. Another silence ensued, and he added, "An eighty-five-degree day in January, huh? I guess it's getting pretty hard to dismiss global warming." Astonishingly, they segued into an ordinary conversation, a conversation that under normal circumstances, with anyone else, would have given her tired face. He had ordered shrimp risotto, and she had ordered salad, and he picked up the check, which seemed unsurprising but still gracious. Also astonishingly, even though the lunch had been worse than she possibly could have imagined, she didn't wish for it to be over; in spite of everything, she liked being in his presence.

Outside, on the sidewalk, in what was obviously their last minute together, he said in a serious voice, "I want to make sure you know"—and she thought he was about to provide consolation—"that it's not like I wish we could be together under different circumstances. I was never romantically interested in you. Never. At all." The sentiment seemed more legalistic than mean, not that the two were mutually exclusive. There was also something legalistic in the way he seemed to be awaiting her acknowledgment.

"Okay," she said.

"You realize, don't you, that you weren't saying what I thought? You were saying what you thought. I was just listening."

"Okay," she said again.

Clearly, they couldn't kiss or hug. He looked at her with trepidation and concern, said, "Take care of yourself," and patted her shoulder.

She watched him retreat down the block, and when he reached the crosswalk, she reentered the lobby of the Four Seasons, found a bathroom, shut herself in a stall, and bawled.

Twenty days had passed since she and Graham had had lunch, and Julie was, when by herself, still crying frequently. This was why, on the morning of chaperoning the field trip to the Butterfly Center, Julie told Lucas's teacher that she needed to pick up a prescription and, instead of riding the bus, would meet them there. Because Julie stopped crying when she passed Dunlavy Street, she had enough time to recover and look mostly normal before joining the students, teachers, and other parents (which, of course, meant other mothers).

In the last three weeks, Julie and Graham had had no contact. Though she'd seen him from a distance at the girls' basketball tournament, they hadn't spoken; the sight of him across the high school gym had made her realize that in the short term, she would miss him as the person she'd lain awake in the middle of the night imagining being naked with, but in the long term what she'd miss was their conversations.

At the natural science museum, Julie parked on the north side. Like the majority of women she knew, she drove an SUV, hers a black BMW. She pulled off her sunglasses before peering at her face in the mirror on the sun visor. Her eyes were only marginally more bloodshot than usual, and her lips, which sometimes swelled when she cried, were their regular size. She put her sunglasses back on and climbed from the car.

The school buses had discharged their freight, and when she joined the throng on the plaza in front of the museum, the second graders were leaping around and jostling one another. Lucas, along with his best friend, Drew, was climbing on a railing on the steps. She waved, and Lucas, who was the most easygoing of her children, waved back; he didn't feel the need to either publicly cling to or ignore her. Many times, with other adults, Julie had winkingly referred to Lucas as her oops baby, because of the age gap between him and his sisters, but she didn't anticipate using the term, with its subtext of sloppy spontaneous marital passion, ever again.

Julie found Mrs. Ackerburg, who was Lucas's teacher.

"Here's your group." Mrs. Ackerburg handed Julie a piece of paper with a typed list of names on it and added, "I've paired you with Gayle Nelson."

Julie hoped her sunglasses concealed her dismay: She hadn't known that Graham's wife—or ex-wife, depending on what stage of the divorce proceedings they were in—would be here. Gayle definitely hadn't been part of the group emails Mrs. Ackerburg had sent. Aloud, Julie said, "Great," then looked around to locate Gayle. Sure enough, she was standing near her daughter Macy.

Julie pretended she hadn't seen her and approached Lucas. "Hey, squirt," she said, and he said, "Hi, Mom." Lucas was four feet tall, with blond curls.

"We were out of cheddar, so I put Swiss on your sandwich for lunch today," she said. "Just so you're not surprised."

"Okay," Lucas said.

"And there's chips," Julie said. "And an apple."

Lucas looked at her with benign curiosity, and Julie thought that this might be her lowest moment yet— worse than all her lustful daydreams about a man other than her husband, worse than her recent months of preoccupation, worse even than unsuccessfully throwing herself at Graham.

"Darth Vader is stronger than Sidious and Obi-Wan put together," Lucas's friend Drew said. "*And* he survived in the river of lava."

A whistle blew, and the children lined up; Mrs. Ackerburg and the two other second-grade teachers took turns reading names aloud so the kids knew where to stand.

Gayle appeared next to Julie and murmured, "There's something I want to ask you."

Julie tried to sound neutral as she said, "Sure." She had no idea whether Gayle had ever suspected anything; it was possible she hadn't and also possible that Gayle had suspected before Julie herself did. But Julie doubted that Graham had told her about their lunch.

"This spring is Mrs. Ackerburg's twenty-fifth anniversary at the school," Gayle said. "Paula and Jen and I were thinking all the families in the class should go in on a gift certificate, but do you think she'd rather have one to a restaurant or a spa?"

"Oh," Julie said. "Well, you could split the difference, right? And do both? I'm happy to contribute."

"If it were me, I'd prefer the spa. I think Sanctuary is really nice."

It was like cortisol—or something—had been released into Julie's bloodstream in preparation for a showdown, and though the cortisol had proved unnecessary, she was compelled to deploy it. She said, "Gayle, how are you doing? In terms of, you know, Graham?" Even now, there was a certain illicit thrill in saying his name aloud, as if he were a regular person.

Gayle rolled her eyes. "Have you heard that he's moved in with Beth? He was staying at a residential hotel for a while, but now he's at her place. Frankly, I'm not sure what *she* sees in *him*. What does a gorgeous thirty-year-old woman want with a man having a midlife crisis?"

Julie's heartbeat had picked up. "Who's Beth?"

"Beth Brenner," Gayle said. "In mergers and acquisitions."

Julie had a dim idea of who this was—an employee of the firm where both Graham and Keith worked, an up-and-comer who was, if Julie was thinking of the right person, her own physical opposite. Her mental image of Beth Brenner was of a tall, slender blonde wearing a short-skirted business suit and high heels.

"I'm sorry," Julie said, which of course was true.

Gayle shook her head. "He claims it started after we

separated, but come *on*. You know what, though? She can have him."

Because the children and adults were entering the museum in a horde, it wasn't the moment for Julie to burst into tears again, though there was time to discreetly check her phone and confirm that Beth Brenner was who she was picturing. Half the second graders were led to the Butterfly Center proper—basically a tropical greenhouse—and the other half, including Lucas's group, started in a classroom, where they were each given a sheet of orange paper that read, across the top, THE WORLD HAS MANY BUTTERFLIES. Below that were the words *Did you know* . . . and an assortment of facts: Butterflies have four wings, fold them when resting, and live during their pupal stage in a chrysalis.

A docent led a discussion among the children while Julie and the other adults stood against a side wall. *She can have him.* Would Julie ever in casual conversation say that about her husband and another woman? It felt unlikely. She had wondered, in retrospect, if she had been hoping to leave Keith for Graham, hoping she and Graham would marry. She thought but wasn't certain that she'd only been trying to have an affair. Though how embarrassing, in light of the news about Beth Brenner, that Julie had imagined Graham might desire her forty-four-year-old self, even boob-lifted and hair-straightened. Sometimes, in the last few weeks, she had thought maybe he'd been denying his attraction to her as an act of chivalry, in order not to destroy her marriage, too. But Beth Brenner offered rather convincing evidence that he'd said he was never romantically interested in her because he was never romantically interested in her.

The children made butterflies out of paper, glitter, and pipe cleaners, and Lucas tried to give her his to hold as they left the classroom. Julie shook her head. "You can hang on to it like everyone else," she said.

In front of the doors to the "rain forest," Julie, Gayle, and the ten children in their group were told by another docent that they should not touch the butterflies, even if one landed on them. Before exiting, they'd need to make sure no butterflies were clinging to their clothes. Already, Julie could feel the humid air.

Julie had been to the Butterfly Center several times. Inside its tropical clime, a walkway snaked around massive nectar plants and fruit trees, below a three-story roof of windowpanes. At first, the children shouted out on glimpsing a butterfly—someone identified a zebra butterfly, then a green swallowtail—but they were so plentiful that the children soon settled down.

And yet, Julie thought, the world did *not* have many butterflies. Or at least for her, it hadn't. A long time ago, after Julie and Keith had been dating for a month, they'd gone for drinks one night with a bunch of his business school classmates, and the next morning, while the two of them were still in bed at Keith's apartment, Julie had begun describing her impressions of his friends—that guy James had been a blowhard, and Ross had made a weird comment about affirmative action, and clearly Nick's girlfriend was anorexic or bulimic or both; in fact, Julie wondered if she'd puked in the bathroom at the bar, because she'd been gone twenty minutes and returned to the table wobbly and minty-smelling.

From his side of the bed, Keith had said, without looking at her, "It's not that you're wrong. But when you say stuff like this, it makes life a lot less enjoyable."

Julie had felt chastened, which possibly had been his intent, or possibly that was only a by-product and the intent was simply to get her to stop. That she had stopped, and remorsefully rather than petulantly, she'd interpreted as a sign of her own maturity, the maturity of their relationship. That Keith had wanted her to stop she'd interpreted as a sign of his decency.

She was just a few feet from the exit when the butterfly landed on her forearm, on top of the thin sleeve of her white cotton sweater. The butterfly had wings of mostly iridescent blue, edged in black with tiny yellow flecks. She raised her arm, the way she would if another person were about to hook his through hers. She expected this to make the butterfly depart, but it remained in place. "Mom!" said Lucas. "There's a butterfly on your arm! You guys, there's a butterfly on my mom's arm!"

The second graders were ecstatic. They exclaimed to her and one another as they approached, inspecting the insect, and *still* it didn't move. It quivered a little, but it didn't fly away. Gayle, who was also nearby, said, "That's good luck, Julie. You should go buy a lottery ticket."

If there was a kind of person who believed in the magic of butterflies, Julie was not one of them. She had no use for this small moment of ostensible enchantment.

"Or maybe it's that you get to make a wish," Gayle said.

It was rude to stare, Julie knew, but for many seconds, she stared at Gayle anyway, wondering just what it was the other woman imagined she would wish for.

Vox Clamantis in Deserto

I'd seen Rae Sullivan around campus, but it wasn't until early February of our freshman year that I decided I wanted to be like her. This realization happened at Dartmouth's post office, on a Tuesday morning, when I was in line behind her; I was there to buy stamps and she was sending a package. It was a little after nine A.M., a quiet hour, and as the only person working helped the students in front of us, I had plenty of time to scrutinize the package in Rae's arms: a cardboard box addressed to a person named Noah Bishop. Though the rest of Noah Bishop's address was obscured by the angle at which Rae was holding the box, I could see that her handwriting was jagged in a cool way—it was unfeminine—and she'd decorated the borders of the box with patterns reminiscent of an Indian tapestry and the rest of it with erratic hearts drawn in black and maroon Sharpie. The hearts seemed to me unabashedly feminine; also, of course, they implied that Rae, whose name I hadn't known until reading the return address in the box's corner, was sending the package to her boyfriend for Valentine's Day. At that time, the thing I most wished for was a boyfriend. I'd been aiming, unsuccessfully, for a Dartmouth boyfriend, but it seemed even more romantic to have one somewhere else—it implied yearning and passionate reunions. I was nineteen and a virgin, and hadn't so much as kissed anyone since arriving on campus five months before.

Rae was a little taller than I was, wearing corduroy pants, Birkenstock clogs, and a North Face coat that, when she turned after paying, fell open in such a way that it revealed a gray hooded sweatshirt with the word EX-ETER across it in maroon. I couldn't actually see all the letters of EXETER, but I'd been at Dartmouth long enough to recognize the name of a fancy boarding school, even if I was from Des Moines. Over her wavy brown hair, Rae wore a black skullcap.

If you went feature by feature, I don't think anyone would have said she and I particularly resembled each other, but there was something recognizable about her to me, some similarity. Our builds were about the same, our hair the same length, our clothes comparable in their implication of not exactly making an effort, though this was 1994, when almost everyone was making less of an effort. But Rae's way of not making an effort fashion-wise was, like her handwriting, far cooler than mine; mine stemmed more from confusion than indifference and resulted in a wardrobe of unironic colorful sweaters and bleached jeans that were loose but tapered.

I didn't speak to Rae in the post office. But that night, after I took off my sweater—it was a cotton crewneck with alternating squares of turquoise, orange, and black—

I never put it back on. I resolved that in the future, I'd wear only solids.

In the fall term of the following year, Rae and I ended up in the same English seminar. I knew from having looked her up in the freshman book—a forest-green paperback booklet filled with black-and-white head shots, with full names and home addresses listed underneath—that she was my year and was from Manchester, New Hampshire. When all of us in the seminar went around the room and introduced ourselves, she said she was an English major. I was pre-med, referred to at Dartmouth as pre-health. Although things still weren't great for me socially, I liked my classes, both the sciences and the humanities, and my grades were good. Partly because I'd been a diligent student in high school and my work habits were ingrained and partly because I didn't know what else to do with myself, I studied a lot.

As a freshman, I'd been assigned a single, which was unusual but not unheard of. For me, it had been disastrous. In the new setting of college, I didn't know how to integrate myself with other people. I had spent a tremendous amount of high school, even while I was studying, thinking about how badly I wanted to go to Dartmouth and about the boyfriends I'd have there. I hadn't realized how much time I'd devoted to my imaginary, longed-for life at Dartmouth until I arrived at Dartmouth and found that by achieving my goal I had lost my primary means of entertaining myself and feeling optimistic. My father, who was a rheumatologist, had himself graduated from Dartmouth in the early seventies, and my family had driven from Iowa to attend his tenth reunion when I was eight, whereupon I had developed a decade-long fixation with the school that was almost romantic in its intensity.

When I started college, my father had been the one to accompany me to campus—this time we flew, changing planes in Chicago—and prior to classes, I'd attended a freshman orientation camping trip in the White Mountains. The night after the trip ended, several girls on my hall assembled by the stairwell to walk to a fraternity party; it was a minor triumph that I'd managed to attach myself to this group. As we descended the steps, the girl in front, a very pretty blond tennis player from Washington, D.C., named Annabel, called over her shoulder, "I heard they call this the GFU party." She paused, then added merrily, "Short for Get Fucked Up."

There were eight or nine girls in the group, and I was bringing up the rear. When I froze, I'm sure no one noticed. I stood there while they descended another flight, and then I returned to my room and lay on my bed and listened to a Garth Brooks CD (my father and I had attended two of his concerts together) and eventually pulled out the MCAT study guide I sometimes looked at before bed; it was a five-hundred-page eight-by-eleven paperback, and something about it was very comforting to me. The girls did, apparently, notice my absence eventually, because the next day one of them said, "Where did you go last night? We all were wondering!" I said I'd felt sick, which in a way I had. For my entire freshman year, I didn't set foot in a fraternity house or, for that matter, a sorority house.

Over the summer, in Des Moines, I spent mornings

babysitting for a family with two little boys and after-
noons volunteering at the hospital where my father
worked. On my bedside table I kept a list of concrete
things I could do to improve my life at Dartmouth,
which included:

-Once a week if someone seems nice and approach-
 able ask if they want to go out for pizza at EBA's
-At least say hi to but try to also smile at people I
 pass
-Join the debate team?

Back on campus, I lived in a single again, and as I
pulled sheets over the twin mattress for the first time, I
wondered, but not optimistically, if this was the bed
where I'd lose my virginity.

As it happened, I didn't join the debate team, and I
didn't execute my EBA's pizza initiative because, after
the very first English seminar, I was leaving the classroom
in Sanborn House when a female voice behind me said,
"What a douchebag." There was a boy walking not with
but parallel to me, about five feet away, and we made
confused eye contact, unsure if the comment was addressed to either or both of us.

When I looked over my shoulder, I saw that the
speaker was Rae Sullivan. In a disgruntled but chummy
tone, as if we'd previously had many similar conversations, she added, "I heard he was full of himself, but his
arrogance exceeded my wildest expectations." She was
referring, I assumed, to the seminar instructor. Although
it was a literature class, he had started by telling us he was
a poet and spent fifteen minutes describing his work.

He'd called it language poetry, a term I had never heard. But I hadn't been bothered by the personal digression; I'd found it impressive.

"I read one of his poems, and it's literally about having anal sex with his wife," Rae was saying. "And I've seen her, and she's a total cow."

I said, "I'm taking the class to fulfill the English requirement." This was as close as I could get to disparaging a professor.

The boy, who had introduced himself in class as Isaac, said, "I found the poems in his first book derivative of Ashbery."

Rae looked between Isaac and me, intensely, for a few seconds, as if making a decision, then said, "Do you guys want to go smoke a joint?"

After Rae and Isaac and I became best friends, it occurred to me only occasionally to wonder whom we were replacing. Who had been Rae's previous best friends? I somehow knew that her freshman roommate had been a girl named Sally Alexander, but she and Sally didn't seem to hang out anymore. Much like my freshman-year neighbor Annabel, she of the GFU party, Sally was blond and very pretty; on the Dartmouth campus, there was a disproportionate number of blond and very pretty girls, socially adept girls, sometimes gracefully anorexic or anorexic-ish girls. I'd observed several who ate no fat, ever; for breakfast, they had a bagel, for lunch a bagel and salad without dressing, and for dinner a bagel, salad without dressing, and frozen yogurt. Not that I witnessed it, but they apparently drank a lot of beer; as a freshman, I had found the term *boot and rally* so anthropologically interesting that I'd shared it with my parents, thereby disturbing my mother. I had a strong sense that, among these poised, preppy, winsomely eating-disordered girls, I couldn't compete for male attention; faced with the enticements of such creatures, what boy would want my dowdy Iowan virginity?

Like me, Rae avoided fraternity parties, which at Dartmouth in 1994 meant avoiding parties. Unexpectedly, she too had a single—hers was in Allen House—and in the evening, after dinner, she liked to sit on her bed, roll and smoke a joint, and watch a VHS tape of *Edward Scissorhands* on her TV. I'd usually leave just before the part of the movie when the housewife tried to seduce Edward, because it stressed me out on behalf of both Edward and the housewife. We were often joined by Isaac, who had grown up in Atlanta and whom I intuitively understood to be gay and closeted. He was short, slim, black haired, and excellent at participating in long, analytical discussions of Rae's two favorite topics, which were her relationship with her boyfriend and people on the Dartmouth campus she hated. In retrospect, I realize that I learned a lot from Isaac about the art of conversation—asking specific follow-up questions, offering non-sycophantic compliments (sycophantic never seemed sincere), and showing patience in the face of repetitive subject matter. Unlike me, Isaac did share Rae's joints; I'd tried a few times, felt like possibly I was smoking wrong and definitely I was reaping no clear benefit, worried about the short- and long-term impacts on my memory, and declined from that point on, which neither of them seemed to mind.

One surprising discovery I made in the first week of

my friendship with Rae was that her boyfriend—Noah Bishop, recipient of the Valentine's Day care package—was younger than she was. He was a junior at Exeter, which meant that she had begun dating him when she was a boarding school senior and he was a freshman. Although Rae revealed this fact without fanfare or embarrassment, I found it so jarring that that night, when Isaac and I left her room at the same time, I said outside her dorm, "Do you think it's weird that she's three years older than Noah?"

"Obviously, the norms of high school imply yes," Isaac said. "But it wouldn't be weird if their genders were reversed. And it wouldn't be that weird if they were a married couple, and she was fifty-three and he was fifty."

I took this in as we walked. Isaac was so much more articulate than I was that I might have found him intimidating, if not for the fact that he was nice; though he'd make damning observations about people, he seemed to be simply stating facts rather than relishing their weaknesses. I said, "Did you go to public or private school?"

"Public."

"Me, too," I said. "And I picture boarding schools being very, like—" I couldn't find the word.

"Conformist?" he asked.

"Yeah. Which would have made them going out even weirder." We kept walking—it was getting dark, and I felt the particular longing of an Ivy League campus at dusk and wished I were walking with a boyfriend of my own instead of with Isaac—and I added, "Although Noah *is* really cute." Indeed, in photographs Rae had shown us, Noah was almost unbearably handsome, in exactly the way I wanted him to be: curly brown hair and full lips and a tiny silver hoop in his left ear. Apparently his family lived in a huge house in Marblehead, Massachusetts, his parents disliked Rae, and he played ice hockey and the guitar. And he had lost his virginity to Rae, though she had lost hers to the son of a friend of her mom's.

If I was offering Isaac an opportunity to formally reveal his gayness, he declined it. He laughed and said, "I bet Noah himself agrees with you."

As the weeks passed, Rae became increasingly concerned that Noah was hooking up with a girl in his class whose name I secretly loved: Clementine Meriwether. In mid-October, Rae decided to pay Noah a visit, which would entail taking the hour-and-a-half bus ride from Hanover to Manchester, then borrowing her mother's car to make the forty-minute drive to Exeter. She invited both Isaac and me to go with her and stay at her mother's house for the weekend; Isaac said he couldn't, but I accepted.

The night before we left, Rae had cramps and asked if I'd pick up dinner for her. As I was leaving the dining hall, carrying a tray with two plates of steaming lasagna and two goblets of vanilla pudding, I pushed open the door to the outside with my back and when I turned around, I was face-to-face with Rae's freshman roommate, Sally Alexander. Sally, who was accompanied by another girl, glanced at the tray and said, in a voice that was more friendly than snotty, though the sentiment seemed snotty, "You're hungry!"

"It's not just for me," I said. "It's for Rae, too."

Sally's eyes narrowed. "Are you friends with her?"

"Yeah," I said, and though I felt a swelling of pride, it was short-lived.

"You don't find her annoying?" Sally said.

Taken aback, I simply said, "No."

Sally shrugged. "She's so self-centered, but I think it's because she's an only child."

Rae's mother's boyfriend picked us up at the bus station in Manchester, after Rae had placed three calls to her mother on a pay phone, and he was fifty minutes late and seemed irritated by our arrival. At her mother's house, which was one story, very small, and brown shingled, he let us off without coming in, then drove on to the office building where he apparently worked nights on the janitorial staff. Rae's mother was a private-duty nurse and wasn't yet finished with her shift. When she did come home, a little after six, wearing pale pink scrubs, she hugged Rae, then hugged me, too, and said how beautiful my eyes were (I'm brown-eyed, and this was a compliment I had never received). She added that she could tell I was an old soul, then asked where I was from and how I liked Dartmouth. She had a thick New Hampshire accent, and both she and the house smelled like cigarette smoke, though the house was generally clean and tidy. We were in Rae's mother's presence for no more than ten minutes before Rae asked her for the car keys.

With an expression of good-natured disappointment, Rae's mother said, "She can't stay away from that boy, can she?" She made me miss my own parents, and it occurred to me to stay there while Rae went to see Noah. I was hungry, and I envisioned eating, say, chicken pot pie with Rae's mother, then perhaps watching *Family Matters* or *Unsolved Mysteries* together before going to bed at ten P.M. But this would be a redux of GFU night, which had set me back God only knew how many months. Thus, reluctantly, I joined Rae in her mother's Honda Civic.

The car was a standard, and I could feel how my earlier self would have been impressed by Rae's casual ability to drive it, seeing her possession of a skill I lacked as in keeping with her general aura of coolness. But there was more and more evidence—starting with the discovery that she was dating someone younger, then reinforced by Sally's comments outside the dining hall—that I'd invented my original idea of Rae, that really, the only person who perceived Rae as cool at all was me. And she hadn't pretended; I had misconstrued. I also, of course, hadn't understood until seeing her mother's house that Rae didn't come from a rich family. Her boarding school degree and her New Englandishly hippie clothes had confused me, because I was easily confused. I realized that, presumably, by Rae's standards if not by my own, I came from a rich family; after all, I had taken out no college loans and was receiving no financial assistance. The decor of my parents' house in Des Moines wasn't that different from the decor of Rae's mother's house—wall-to-wall carpet, faded sofas and chairs, shiny walnut tables—but my parents' house was much bigger.

Rae slipped a cassette into the dashboard tape deck before backing out of the driveway, and the Indigo Girls' song "Joking" erupted into the car; when it ended, she said, "Can you rewind it?" At her request, I did this so many times as we drove east on 101 that I soon knew precisely how long to hold down the button in order to get back to the song's start. "Joking" was on an album I'd heard in Rae's room, and though I wasn't certain what made this song a personal anthem for her—it started with intense guitar strumming—I understood the impulse behind it, the craving.

We'd been driving for twenty minutes when Rae slapped her right hand against the steering wheel and said, "Fuck!"

I glanced across the front seat.

"I forgot the pot," Rae said. "And Noah reminded me, like, three times."

I did not feel optimistic about Rae's reunion with Noah, or about my own ability to comfort her if the reunion was unsuccessful. "Do you want to turn back?"

She thought for a few seconds, then said, "There's not time. He has choir practice at eight."

Hot, pot-smoking Noah Bishop was in the choir?

I had been intrigued by the prospect of visiting an elite boarding school, but I couldn't see much as we arrived under darkness at what seemed to be the back side of a vast concrete gym. A boy in a down vest, a plaid flannel shirt, khaki pants, and sneakers was standing with his back to the gym, under a light, and Rae unrolled her window and wolf-whistled at him.

"Do you have it?" he asked.

"Fuck you," she said out the window. "That's not how you greet me."

She parked in an otherwise empty lot, and we both climbed from the car. Gratifyingly, Noah Bishop was even handsomer than he looked in photographs. She ap-

proached him, placed both hands on his shoulders, and
kissed him on the mouth. When she pulled away, she
said, "*That's* how you greet me."

He gestured toward me. "Who's that?"

"My friend Dana," Rae said.

Noah nodded once and said, "Yo, my friend Dana."

I knew that when Noah ejaculated, he made a whim-
pering noise, like a baby; that when Rae gave him hand
jobs, he liked her to use Jergens lotion; that the first
woman he'd ever masturbated to had been Kelly LeBrock,
after he saw the movie *Weird Science;* and that his father
had been investigated by the SEC and found innocent of
wrongdoing, though Noah himself suspected that his father was guilty. I also knew that sometimes Rae knelt on
the floor of her Dartmouth dorm room, clasped her
hands together, and, addressing the phone on her desk,
said, "Call me, Noah. Just please fucking call me right
now."

"Hi," I said.

"Did you get the key?" Rae asked Noah, and he said,
"Yeah. Did you get the weed?"

"There were complications," she said.

I cleared my throat. "Is town that way? Maybe I'll go
eat dinner. I should be back by, what, eight, Rae? Or
eight-fifteen?"

"Sure," she said, and I could tell she was barely paying
attention.

Even though I made a couple of wrong turns, I reached
the town of Exeter within fifteen minutes and kept walk-

ing until I found a place where I could buy a meatball sub
and a Diet Coke. A handful of kids who looked like students came in, and I reminded myself that the unease I
felt about eating alone at Dartmouth was irrelevant here.
When I finished, I walked along Water Street, not entirely sure what to do. I had no idea, of course, that of all
the feelings of my youth that would pass, it was this one,
of an abundance of time so great as to routinely be unfill-
able, that would vanish with the least ceremony.

The stores, most of which were closed, were brick,
with awnings or quaint wooden signs outside. I entered a
pharmacy. When I found myself in the "family planning"
aisle, I decided, just as an experiment, to buy a pack of
condoms. Would I plausibly seem to the cashier like a
person who was having sex? The wide array—lubricated
and ribbed and ultra-thin—bewildered me, so I went
with what was cheapest. I also picked up a bag of Twizzlers and some lip balm, for camouflage. My heart was
beating quickly as I waited to pay, but when it was my
turn, the cashier seemed as uninterested in me as Noah
had. By then, it was almost eight, so I walked back to the
gym swinging the plastic bag with my purchases in it.

At first, I thought my timing was perfect, because as I
approached the gym, Rae was pulling the Honda out of
its parking space. Then I realized she was pulling out
alarmingly quickly; her tires squealed in a way I had rarely
heard in real life. When the front of the car was pointed
toward the road, she revved the gas and almost ran me
over as she sped past. "Rae!" I yelled. "Rae!"

But the car didn't stop, and its taillights had soon disappeared.

"I guess you're screwed," someone said, and I turned and saw that Noah stood about twenty feet away, smirking.

I walked toward him. "Where's she going?"

He shrugged.

"Is she coming back?"

"Hard to say."

"Did she say she was going to find me?"

He shook his head. "Sorry."

"Did you guys have a fight?" This was a nosier question than I'd have asked under normal circumstances, especially of a good-looking guy, but he was still in high school. Plus, Rae was or had been his girlfriend, and she wasn't prettier than I was. And then I understood, with a weird revelatory kind of internal kick, what had drawn me to Rae in the post office. Since arriving at Dartmouth, I'd felt my own lack of prettiness as a humming, low-level failure. I wasn't singularly unattractive, my existence wasn't a *crime*. But I also wasn't, in an environment of youth and affluence, fulfilling my part of the social contract—the thing it mattered the most if I was, I wasn't. And yet Rae wasn't really fulfilling it, either; Rae wasn't beautiful or blond or thin or charming, and she didn't seem apologetic. Even having lost some of my original respect for her, I still envied her confidence.

Noah said, "She's pissed because I didn't want to fuck her."

I blinked, then said, "Why not?"

Did I think there was useful information to be gleaned here, sexual or romantic lessons, or was I already scheming? Looking back, I'm still not sure.

Shrugging again, he said, "She's on the rag." He grinned as he added, "I told her she could still blow me."

I hesitated, and my heart abruptly began to pound at double or triple time. But I spoke slowly. I said, "*I'm* not on the rag." Although this wasn't a locution I generally used, there was much about the moment that was out of character.

If I'd been hoping that some transporting lust would seize both of us, I would have been disappointed. The expression on Noah's face was a surprised and faintly amused sort of curiosity, as if he was wondering if I'd farted. He raised his eyebrows and said, "Yeah?"

We were, at that point, only about four feet apart. "Yeah," I said. I didn't know what to do next, and I thought of turning and sprinting away. But I again recalled the GFU night, my failure of nerve. Presumably, I needed to touch him, but how? The two times in Des Moines when I'd kissed boys, they'd both initiated it.

The most logical place to make contact with Noah seemed to be the crotch of his pants, but that was too aggressive even for the person I was pretending to be. And kissing him seemed logistically complicated—he was well over six feet, significantly taller than I was, and I wondered how Rae had made it look easy.

From somewhere far away, I heard bells ringing—the eight o'clock bells, followed by the distant, cheerful-sounding, intermittent shouts and cries of teenagers. Instead of having sex with me, was Noah about to depart for choir practice? With both my arms, I reached for his right hand, brought it to my chest, and held it against my left breast, on top of my navy blue sweater. This, apparently, was all I needed to do. There were a few seconds when I thought he was pulling his hand away, which he was, but before my humiliation could be fully activated, he slid the hand back under my sweater and T-shirt, over my bra, and before long he'd slipped his thumb beneath the bra. Then he did kiss me. In spite of his handsomeness, I remained completely unaroused. My lack of arousal did not, however, prevent me from saying, after a minute or two, "Is there somewhere we can go?"

He grabbed my hand and led me inside an unlocked door of the gym and through a corridor. Outside another door, this one maroon, he looked in either direction down the hall before pulling a key from his pocket. The room was windowless and contained soccer balls in vast net bags, bats, stacks of orange traffic cones, and other kinds of athletic equipment. There wasn't much open space on the polished concrete floor, but there was enough for a girl who was five foot four to lie down and for a boy who was a foot taller to lie on top of her. We used one of the condoms I'd just bought at the pharmacy—had any condom purchased outside the heat of passion ever been used so efficiently?—and the whole encounter lasted less than ten minutes, maybe closer to five. None of it was physically enjoyable for me, except when he held my hand to lead me inside the gym; that had been the kind of thing I'd pictured a boyfriend doing. About thirty seconds after coming (as advertised, he did so with a whimper), he said, "I need to go to choir practice," and he rose up off me. We'd both kept our shirts on and hadn't entirely removed our pants. We refastened them, and I smoothed my hair. He opened the door carefully, looked into the hallway, then motioned for me to follow him. Outside the door, he locked it, glanced at me, smirked, and said, "See you around." Then he headed in one direction and, retracing our route in from the parking lot, I headed in the other.

After college, I was a research assistant in a lab in Boston for two years before attending medical school at Johns Hopkins. I matched to my first-choice residency, which was at the University of Iowa, and I was a year into it when I received a phone call from Isaac. I later learned that he had called information in Des Moines to get my parents' phone number, then asked my mother for my number. He was driving cross-country because he was about to start an English PhD program at Berkeley and wanted to know if I'd like to have dinner when he passed through Iowa City the following week. I was working twenty-four-hour shifts, so we met instead for breakfast, at a diner. From the minute I entered the restaurant and saw him sitting in the booth—when we made eye contact, he smiled, waved, and stood—I understood that Isaac was not gay. My heart thudded as we hugged, though I felt more excited than nervous. I was by then almost thirty, and I'd had a few boyfriends and a few additional sexual partners, but I'd never before been able to tell for certain that someone else was as happy to be in my presence as I was to be in his.

In medical school, I'd studied by relistening to first- and second-year class lectures on tape, and I would speed up the lectures, making the professors sound like cartoon chipmunks, in order to get through them as fast as possible. In the diner, I wished I could increase the speed of my conversation with Isaac, not because I wanted to get it over with but because I wanted both of us to cram in the maximum amount of words before I started my shift, because I felt we had such an enormous amount to say to each other.

The great luck of my entire life is that twelve years have passed since Isaac and I had breakfast, and I still feel that way. We live outside Columbus, Ohio, where he is an English professor and I practice internal medicine at a clinic that serves uninsured immigrants. We have a daughter who is now ten and a son who's seven. When we can, we like to go for family walks after dinner in our suburban neighborhood; often our children dart ahead of us, or discuss their own matters with each other, and when Isaac and I chat about our days, or the news, or movies we probably won't end up seeing, I am filled with gratitude at the astonishing fact of being married to someone I enjoy talking to, someone with whom I can't imagine ever running out of things to say.

Isaac claims that he always had a crush on me and that was the reason he hung out in Rae's room, even though he never much liked her. When I told Isaac that I'd believed he was gay, he was amused and asked why, and when I tried to pinpoint it, the best I could come up with was that he'd used gel in his hair, he'd buttoned the top button of his shirts, and I hadn't been uncomfortable around him. He was amused by all of this, too.

It would be easy for me to be horrified by who I was more than twenty years ago, how ignorant, but I don't see what purpose it would serve. I'm relieved to have aged out of that visceral sense that my primary obligation is to be pretty, relieved to work at a job that allows me to feel useful. Did I used to think being pretty was my primary obligation because I was in some way delusional? Or was it that I'd absorbed the messages I was meant to absorb with the same diligence with which I studied? As the mother of a daughter, I hope she won't judge herself as harshly as I judged myself, but her personality is so unlike mine—she is boisterous and outspoken—that I'm not inordinately concerned.

Isaac, as I didn't know back in college, was also a virgin when I met him. It was in sophomore spring that he got together with his first girlfriend, which is to say he had sex after I did but, I trust, more thoroughly. Presumably, the campus of Dartmouth in the early nineties—like college campuses in every decade, like towns and cities everywhere—was home to many other virgins, average-looking girls and boys and also grown-ups afraid that they were too ugly to be loved, convinced that this private shame was theirs alone.

I had thought that extracting myself from my friendship with Rae would be tricky, that she'd resist, but it wasn't and she didn't. That night at Exeter, I waited in the parking lot for more than an hour—because I was amazed by the implications of my nonvirgin status and because I had Twizzlers to eat, I wasn't bored—and finally the Honda Civic reappeared. When I climbed in, Rae expressed no contrition about abandoning me, and we listened many more times to the song "Joking." I wondered if Noah would ever tell her what had happened, and if she'd confront, or even physically accost, me, but of course he had no more incentive to reveal anything than I did. I suspect that they weren't in touch much longer.

All sophomores at Dartmouth stayed on campus and took classes for the summer, and it was at some point in July or August that I realized it had been a long while since I'd laid eyes on Rae, even from a distance. The only conversation I remember having with Isaac at Dartmouth after my trip to Manchester was when I ran into him that summer outside Baker-Berry Library and he confirmed that Rae had dropped out.

These days, Isaac and I almost never talk about Rae, though she crosses my mind with regularity; I'm far more troubled that she probably didn't earn a degree from Dartmouth than that I had sex with her boyfriend. I've found no trace of her online, and in this void, I've created a biography: She works in public relations for a large and mildly nefarious corporation. She's tough and powerful and makes a lot of money. She never wanted children and lives in a swanky apartment in a big city with her good-looking and (I can't resist) slightly younger boyfriend. If you were to mention Isaac or me, she wouldn't know who we were, but, upon consideration, she'd acknowledge that our names sounded vaguely familiar.

Bad Latch

O f the ten of us enrolled in the prenatal yoga class
that summer at the Y, I was the second most pregnant, and the woman who was the most pregnant was
named Gretchen. All of us sat on oversized rubber balls,
and Gretchen always staked out the center of the front
row, closest to the instructor. The first class, when we
were supposed to go around and say our name, due date,
whether we knew if it was a boy or girl, and where we
were planning to deliver, she said August 18—my due
date was August 29—and added, "Carl and I want to be
surprised about the gender, because in our information-
saturated world, it's nice to still allow for some mystery
and magic, right?" She'd turned around on her ball so
she was facing those of us in the second and third rows,
and she smiled self-congratulatorily.

She had a high brown ponytail and wore a mint-green
tank top that stretched over her belly and cost sixty-two
dollars, which I knew because I'd seen it at a maternity
boutique full of clothes I couldn't afford. "We're de-

livering at home with a midwife," Gretchen continued. "Drug-free and all that. And then I'll be a stay-at-home mom because it's like, if you're going to outsource your childcare, why even bother to become a parent in the first place?"

Lest it seem like this class occurred in a place where you could get away with saying such things—Brooklyn, maybe, or Berkeley?—it didn't. It occurred in Omaha, Nebraska, and I heard Gretchen repeat her comments verbatim—*Carl, information-saturated, mystery, magic, home birth, drug-free, outsource*—every Saturday morning for the next five weeks because the instructor liked us to reintroduce ourselves each time. The sixth class, Gretchen wasn't there. Her absence meant that when we discussed which parts of our bodies were newly sore or swollen, a discussion Gretchen had consistently dominated, my concerns took precedence over everyone else's.

At the end of class, as we lay under nubbly Mexican blankets while the instructor guided us on a visualization of our peaceful, joyous deliveries, I wondered how Gretchen's home birth had gone. Or perhaps she was in labor at that very moment, simultaneously snacking on organic trail mix and breathing mindfully as stalwart Carl massaged her hips.

As for me, at the grocery store, strangers would look at my belly and say, "Any minute now!" Then at five A.M. on a hot Thursday, after a bunch of contractions, an epidural, a lot of pushing, and a lot more pushing, she arrived; we had known in advance she'd be a girl, and we'd decided to call her Sadie. Everything about her was otherworldly and astonishing: Her eyes were big and brown, her nose was tiny and upturned, and her mouth was set in a nonplussed purse. "She looks mad," I said, and my husband, Adam, who was choked up, said, "We have a daughter."

It was a month later that I saw Gretchen again, this time at the weekly breast-feeding support group hosted by the maternity boutique whose clothes I couldn't afford. By then Sadie was sleeping at night in a carpeted cat box between Adam and me, and we'd removed everything but the fitted sheet from our bed, all in an effort to get some rest while not smothering her. Also, I was finding nursing unbearable. The moment of her clamping on was like someone biting your skinned knee, and whenever she turned her head toward my chest, rooting, I was filled with dread. Intermittently, I'd place huge green cabbage leaves on my boobs, between my bra and skin, a recommendation I'd read on a website, though I'd yet to experience any decrease in soreness.

Adam had returned to his office a week after Sadie's birth. I, meanwhile, would have a three-month maternity leave before resuming my job four days a week, one of which I'd work from home. On the days I couldn't be with Sadie, Adam's mother would come to our house to babysit. Although my job was considerably less cool than what I'd once imagined doing with my life—my employer was a multinational food manufacturer that, as it happened, was the number one seller of infant formula, which I wasn't planning to use—my flexible childcare arrangement made me feel as if seven years with the company and a good relationship with my boss were paying off.

The breast-feeding support group occurred in a room accessed by a curtained-off doorway at the rear of the boutique. Despite the swankiness of the boutique's merchandise, this room was filled with furniture whose best days had come and gone: Three mismatched, stained couches and a handful of chairs formed a lopsided circle. Scattered about were those C-shaped pillows I had believed until shortly before Sadie's birth were meant to alleviate the discomfort of hemorrhoids but now knew were platforms for nursing babies. When I entered the room, eleven or twelve other women, all with infants, were chatting, about half of them with their breasts fully or partially displayed; instead of being differentiated by their personalities, the women were differentiated by their nipples. I'd carried Sadie inside in her car seat, and I set it on the floor behind an empty chair, along with her diaper bag, and lifted her out.

Mother-baby duos continued to trickle in as the support group's leader, a gorgeous and slender woman wearing a crocheted turquoise sundress, got things rolling. "I'm Niko," she said. "I'm the mom of Scarlett, who's six and has self-weaned, and Declan, who's four and loves breast-feeding. I'm passionate about helping moms like you give this beautiful, natural, and super-healthy gift to your little ones."

As with prenatal yoga, we were then supposed to go around and introduce ourselves. Gretchen went third, and after she'd said her name she said, "And this is Piper, who was born via C-section after a grueling twenty-six hours of labor. I was like, 'No drugs! No drugs!' and Carl was like, 'Gretchen, seriously, you're superwoman,' but then there was an umbilical cord prolapse, so it was out of my hands. On the upside, Piper's nursing like a champ."

"If your delivery didn't happen how you wanted, it's important to grieve," Niko said. "At the same time, don't underestimate how amazing it is that now you're literally sustaining her with your own body."

The next person who introduced herself was named Jessica, her baby was Ethan, and both of them began to cry as Jessica described how challenging Ethan's tongue-tie made breast-feeding, which caused me to perk up with interest. Introductions were then stalled for twenty minutes as other mothers murmured support and a discussion of positions occurred. Niko was soon on her knees crouched over Jessica, maneuvering Jessica's left breast, though she looked around at all of us as she said, "Breast-feeding shouldn't hurt. We wouldn't have survived as a species if it did, right? So if you're in pain, what it probably means is that you have a bad latch."

Introductions never did get all the way around the circle, and the hour was finished—it concluded with Niko reading aloud a poem that rhymed *lactation* and *revelation*—before I'd said my own or Sadie's name. I set my daughter back in her car seat, hoisted the diaper bag onto my shoulder, took all of us out to the car, and drove home, stopping on the way to purchase a 1.45-pound container of powdered formula. Fixing Sadie a bottle that afternoon felt at first like a transgression and then, as she accepted it unfussily, like a relief. I planned to alternate between formula and breast milk, but within a week, I'd stopped nursing altogether and was using my employee coupons to buy formula in bulk; needless to say, I didn't return to the support group.

The third place I crossed paths with Gretchen was at infant swim lessons. By that point, Sadie was six months old. The lessons occurred on Tuesday mornings, which was the day I "worked" from home, though my original plan to get things done while Sadie napped had been delusional and I'd basically given up on it. To seem productive, I sent frequent emails to my co-workers.

Only five babies were enrolled in the swim class, but if Gretchen recognized me, she gave no sign of it. A strange intimacy existed between us as we stood in the water next to each other in our tank bathing suits or took turns holding our babies in the center of the circle while singing. ("Purple potatoes, and purple tomatoes, and *Sadie* is in the stew!") Yet Gretchen and I never spoke to each other directly. Piper seemed good-natured, and I assumed that she was still nursing like a champ and that Gretchen was greatly enjoying not outsourcing her childcare.

Then, around the fourth class, Gretchen and Piper stopped showing up. The weird part was that I almost missed them. Without the tension created by my antipathy toward Gretchen, the half hour felt slack, and I realized for the first time that I found the swim lessons boring.

Another three months passed, during which my company laid off twelve hundred employees, including my boss and five other people in my department. My new boss was a twenty-six-year-old guy with an MBA—that is, he was three years younger than I was—and he told me that if I wanted to keep my job, I needed to work full-time and on-site. The next day, my mother-in-law, who'd been walking with a limp for two years, was approved by her orthopedist to have her hip replaced; her recovery would last four to six weeks, and taking care of Sadie during that time was out of the question.

It wasn't that I looked down on parents who put their

kids in daycare, it wasn't that I *disapproved* of them, or at least if I did disapprove, I knew enough to be embarrassed by my disapproval. I wasn't a person compelled to broadcast my own choices in the hopes of making other people feel inferior. Nevertheless, on Sadie's first day at Green Valley Children's Center, I didn't even make it out the front door before I burst into tears. I hadn't felt that bad about some of the things that women having babies when I did, even in Omaha, were supposed to feel bad about—an epidural, formula—but the collapse of my carefully crafted childcare setup seemed like a failure of a different magnitude.

Although Adam and I had planned to bring Sadie to daycare together, a last-minute meeting had been scheduled at his office, so I was alone. Blinded by tears, I pushed open the front door of the center and stood in the parking lot, sobbing. I needed to get to my car, to hide, but I was so flustered that I couldn't remember where I'd parked.

And then someone's arms were around me—the someone was female, and her shampoo smelled like coconut—and she was saying, "It's your first day, right? I saw you doing drop-off upstairs. But don't worry, because, seriously, Green Valley is great. I was nervous, too, but now I love it so much."

It took several seconds of collecting myself, and then of focusing on the woman's face—she was still embracing me, and we were almost too close together for me to see her—to realize that the woman was Gretchen. I think she understood that I was recognizing her—perhaps I flinched—and she dropped her arms. She said, "I don't know if you remember me, but we were in the same—"

"I remember you." I wiped my nose with my left palm. "I thought you were a stay-at-home mom."

She laughed. "Well, Carl left me in March, which kind of threw a wrench into things." Then she said, "It turns out my husband was having an affair since before I got pregnant, and now I'm single and working full-time. Life is full of surprises, huh?" I was taken aback and said nothing, and she added, "Really, though, I've been so happy with this place. I've learned a ton from the teachers."

It was early July, almost a full year since Gretchen and I had met, although in a way we'd never met. Neither of our daughters had celebrated their first birthdays yet, and when I look back—our girls are eight now—I'm struck by how that was still the beginning of them becoming themselves and of us becoming mothers. In the years since, Sadie and Piper have learned to tie their shoes and ride bikes and read. They've had croup and stomach flu, their feelings have been hurt, they've lost teeth, they've performed in ballet recitals. I don't know if it's more improbable that Gretchen and I became each other's closest friends or that our daughters did, too. Not that it's all been easy for any of us—I had two miscarriages before the birth of my son, and Gretchen got engaged again but subsequently called it off. Sometimes when I see photos Adam took of me holding Sadie in the first month of her life, I can discern the faintly bumpy outline of cabbage leaves beneath my nursing bra, and I'm reminded of a particular kind of confusion that hasn't entirely disappeared but has, with time, decreased.

That morning in the parking lot, I sniffled once more, then extended my hand to Gretchen. "Hi," I said. "I'm Rachel."

Plausible Deniability

"Stop me if I've told you this," my brother says. "Libby read an article about how when you flush the toilet, tons of germs shoot up and coat everything nearby."

"You've told me this," I say.

"When she takes a shit, she's started putting on a special T-shirt so that her regular clothes don't touch the back of the toilet. But is she, like, *nestling* against the lid? She's in the bathroom every morning way longer than I am, so maybe."

"You've told me this," I say again.

"Here's the thing. If you're an adult, whatever happens in there is between you and your god. Right? But she fuckin' announces all this to me, and she's even given the shirt a name—it's her poop shirt. She hangs it on the back of the bathroom door next to our robes, this random pink T-shirt, and every time I see it, it's like she's rubbing my face in it."

"In the toilet germs?" I ask.

"In the disgustingness of her humanity. Does she *want* me to cheat?"

It is six thirty-three on a Friday morning in February, about forty degrees, and still dark. We're running east on Pershing toward Forest Park. On Monday, Wednesday, and Friday, I leave my apartment at six-twenty and get to Mark's house by six-thirty. They live in a brick colonial—stately on the outside, cluttered and dog-hair-filled when you step in—and if he's already stretching in the drive-way when I arrive, it usually means he awakened before his alarm went off and is in a bad mood. If I have to text him because he's still inside, maybe still asleep, it means he's equanimous. Occasionally, it even means he and Libby had sex the night before.

"I doubt the shirt has anything to do with you," I say. "I think she's just existing." I add, "She doesn't want you to cheat, Mark. Don't cheat."

Though my brother is next to me and I'm not looking at his face, I know his exact expression as he mutters, "Said like a man who's never been married."

It's while I'm parking in the garage adjacent to my law firm—I live in the suburb of Clayton and work in downtown St. Louis—that I feel, in my pocket, the ping of an incoming email. When I glance at the screen of my phone, I can see the first sentence, but I postpone reading the entire message. This way, an anticipatory pleasure—if I am being honest, the purest pleasure of my life these days—imbues the otherwise mundane six minutes it takes to ride the garage elevator to the lobby, cross the lobby to the other bank of elevators, and rise to the fifth floor, where I'm deposited at the glass entrance of Grant, Molyneux, and Molyneux.

I greet Gloria at the front desk and my assistant, Rosemary, outside my office, set my briefcase on the desk, sit, and read the email on my phone; the phone's smaller screen feels more intimate than my computer. Like almost all the others, the message is one paragraph, with neither greeting nor sign-off; rather, it ends with a YouTube link.

Even as a child, I remember being enraptured by this piece—how the long orchestra statement of the first theme builds and builds in excitement and then the violin and viola enter in octaves in a seemingly random moment. When I was younger, I thought it sounded like how flying would feel. And the second movement has to be some of Mozart's most beautiful and sad music ever—apparently, he wrote it shortly after his mom died.

The link is to Itzhak Perlman and Pinchas Zukerman playing the *Sinfonia Concertante in E-flat Major for Violin, Viola and Orchestra,* conducted by Zubin Mehta. It was recorded in 1982 with the Israel Philharmonic Orchestra and is twenty-five minutes long, and I am seven minutes in when I hear someone saying my name.

"William?" It is Rosemary, standing at the threshold. "Richard Reinhardt from Brevature is holding for you."

"We went out for dinner on Saturday with the Kleins," Mark says. "One of those standard two-couple snoozefests, but primates are wired to socialize, right? Why fight it?"

It's Monday, and, as it happens, I had dinner last night at Mark and Libby's, as I do most Sundays: I played basketball in the driveway with my nephews, who are ten and thirteen, and, after the meal, I was praised by Libby for loading the dishwasher, which Mark never does. But in the presence of his wife and children, Mark jokes around a lot and reveals little.

As we make a left from Big Bend onto Forsyth, I ask, "Where'd you guys eat?"

He says Parigi, a new, expensive place that serves French-Italian fusion. "The four of us split a few bottles of wine." This detail catches my attention, but I say nothing, and Mark continues: "We got home, I checked on the kids, and, miracle of miracles, they were both asleep. I told Libby she looked nice. I start to kiss her, and she says, 'Just so you know, there's a zero percent chance we're having sex tonight.'" He laughs mirthlessly. "Zero percent! She claimed she'd eaten too much, but I think she was pissed because I'd said at dinner that Sandra Bullock is annoying."

I roll my eyes. "Sandra Bullock is America's sweetheart."

"You sound like Libby." He shrugs. "I have opinions. Sue me."

"Maybe Libby *had* eaten too much."

"You know when I realized she'd given up on me? When she started preferring doggy-style. That used to be, like, a present, for special occasions, but she wanted missionary as our go-to—gazing into each other's eyes and all that crap. Now she's fine with me getting her off with my hand, then before I can even ask, she's on her knees with her ass in the air. And don't get me wrong, for sure it's efficient, but it's like, who's she picturing while I'm behind her?"

"If you get her off with your hand, isn't it likelier that *that's* when she's picturing someone else?"

After a pause, with a degree of fondness, Mark says, "Sometimes you're a real prick."

When I turned forty, which was sixteen months ago, I expected that the pressure to marry—the pressure exerted by others—would intensify, but to my surprise, it decreased. It turned out that simply by celebrating this particular birthday, I'd crossed some border of nonconformity, and while I still could—can—turn around, retrace my steps, and assume citizenship in the nation of wedlock, the expectation seems to be that I won't. I now hear, in reference to myself, the word *bachelor;* and though it evokes an image of a fussy gay man, and though I'm not gay and choose to believe I'm not fussy, either, I don't mind. In fact, I'm relieved. I've dated plenty of women—nearly all of them intelligent and attractive, some exceptionally so—and I've never wanted to permanently attach my life to theirs; I've never even come close enough to be able to pretend to want it. That I understood our alliances to be temporary while the women were more optimistic was, as I progressed through my thirties, an increasingly keen source of pain—for the women, obviously, but for me, too. In one case, at my girlfriend's behest, I read two books about men who fear commitment. But my feelings didn't change. My aversion to the prospect of a spouse and children was, apparently, anomalous enough that it needed an explanation, and I'm pretty sure this need was exacerbated by my appearance. I was average when younger—like Mark, I have red hair, which has faded in intensity, and skin covered in ginger freckles—but just as the passage of time changed the meaning of my being single, it changed the value of my looks; and as the years passed without my putting on weight or losing much hair, I attained some higher status of desirability, enhanced, no doubt, by making partner at Grant, Molyneux, and Molyneux. That is, I've remained myself while my currency has increased.

Mark, who at forty-three is just under two years older than I am, got married when he was twenty-six, the summer after he'd finished medical school. Libby had been his college girlfriend and worked in private school admissions until their first child was born, and she resumed that role when their second started kindergarten. That Mark's a pediatric cardiologist mostly offsets—to me, if not to everyone—how he's also kind of an asshole. Meanwhile, I consider myself morally neutral. I practice bankruptcy, restructuring, and creditors' rights law, and, yes, I routinely represent clients widely agreed to be the bad guys, but I also do pro bono work, including teaching a quarterly "financial literacy" class at a nonprofit. So: a wash.

Even as I resist the idea that my singleness requires more explanation than Mark's seventeen-year marriage, there was an explanation I offered to my girlfriends and happen to believe, disappointing as it is in both its succinctness and its banality. My parents had a bad divorce; the almost two additional years that Mark spent experiencing their marriage before it soured were, it seems, crucial in allowing him to later suspend disbelief about the institution. Or you could just chalk it up to our being different people.

It's slightly less clear to me that I never wanted children than it is that I never wanted to marry, but I mostly didn't, and in any case, Finn and Noah charm me on

Sunday evenings without leaving me regretful when I depart from their house.

Mark and I are passing the baseball fields of Washington University when I say, "Seriously, though—I'm sure Libby hasn't given up on you." Mark says nothing, and I ask, "So was Parigi any good?"

"It was okay." When I glance at him, Mark smirks. "The food was a little rich."

I like how slow and powerful this piece is, I write. *It amazes me how much emotion Chopin could fit into something that's only four and a half minutes. (You probably already know people called this "Sadness.") Is it weird that Chopin and the Pixies remind me of each other? It's how they both move so quickly and effectively from loud to quiet.*

The link I attach is to Étude op. 10, no. 3.

I text Bonnie at six, while I'm still at the office: *Feel like company tonight?*

Her response arrives less than a minute later: *Sorry I have Sophia*

Bonnie and I met seven months ago, through a dating app, though *dating* is of course a euphemism. She lives twenty-five minutes south of me, is the manager of a housewares store—it's part of a national chain, and hers is at a mall—and is divorced, with a nine-year-old daughter I've never met. We see each other every ten days or so, and though we went out for drinks a few times in the beginning, our encounters now occur exclusively inside my apartment or her condo and start at around 8:30

P.M., with a glass of wine and a discussion of current events; we share few other frames of reference. After sex, she stays over, which I don't mind, but I never stay at her condo. I usually fall asleep, then wake at midnight or one and drive home.

Bonnie is pretty enough—she's thirty-eight, with obviously dyed long black hair—and the curviest woman I've been involved with. She must outweigh me by thirty pounds, and I'm reminded, when she's straddling me, of the middle school girls who entered puberty before the boys did. The truth is that I consider her a kind of preventive medicine. If I could make my libido disappear, I would, and as I age, this might well happen; certainly it's decreased already. But it hasn't yet gone away, and I've found in the past that I can go without sex for three or four months, and then one day I wake up in despair. Presumably, there are biological explanations, and my abrupt desperation has as much to do with touch as sex, meaning maybe I could stave it off with massages, of the more or less sordid varieties. I'm considering trying this after Bonnie tires of me, which I imagine will happen when she decides she wants a real relationship, a stepfather for her daughter. I will lament such a development and do nothing to stop it. *No worries,* I text back.

At six forty-five, I leave the office, drive to Clayton, park outside my apartment building, and walk to a restaurant where, once or twice a week, I have dinner at the bar. The bartender, who is French and whose name is Thérèse, is the woman I currently am most attracted to; if she and Bonnie were standing side by side, Bonnie might not appear pretty enough after all. And if I were younger and knew less about myself, I'd pursue Thérèse.

Even now, though I'm fifteen years older than she is, I have a feeling she'd accept if I asked her out. She's unfailingly warm and has remarked more than once on how unusual it is that I pronounce her name correctly. Despite the two accent marks that appear on her name tag, apparently most St. Louisans pronounce it not only with a long second *e*, but also with a nonexistent *a* on the end.

I take a seat on a stool and Thérèse smiles and says, "William." Ironically, she mispronounces my name—she says Weel-yum—and I find it very endearing.

I ask for a whiskey and soda, which Thérèse deposits in front of me with two skinny black straws and a curl of lemon rind. For dinner, I order green salad with wild salmon, and she says, in a teasing voice, "Always so healthy."

"Not always," I say, though I do avoid bread and sugar. It's when I'm eating with others, most frequently with Mark's family, that I relent, more as a matter of politeness than indulgence.

"But you are not the only one," Thérèse says in her beguiling accent. "I now train for a triathlon." She holds up both her arms—despite the chilly temperature outside, she is wearing a tight sleeveless black top—and flexes her biceps.

"Impressive," I say. "When is it?"

"April. You run, yes?"

"I do run. With my brother."

"Maybe someday you and I run together." She raises both eyebrows, in the playful manner of a woman aware of how attractive she is.

When it becomes clear that she's waiting for a response, I say—I make sure to say it pleasantly—"Maybe so."

She then turns to attend to a couple on another of the

bar's three sides—there are only twelve seats around the bar, most empty on this Tuesday night—but instead of admiring her small, toned ass and graceful stance, as I usually would, I feel a dismal sorrow. She ruined it. It happened so quickly, but now it's finished. Though she asked me out with a casual deftness that allows us both to pretend she didn't, she did. And I'm certain that the intermittent rhythm of interacting with Thérèse while she's on the clock is far more enjoyable than her unbroken attention on a date would be.

It's also true that if she were less fluent in English, I'd probably have asked her out, weeks ago, in spite of everything; we could coast longer on each other's mystery. But the language barrier is negligible. If I did ask her out, I don't doubt that after the initial exuberance, I'd be quietly bored, politely restless, possibly subjected to reading yet another book about men who fear commitment. And Thérèse is young and lovely. She deserves better.

It is, I assume, due to her confidence that she doesn't comprehend until after I've signed the check and am standing that I'm not going to follow up on her overture; I won't try to confirm a day or time for us to run together, even tentatively. First, she's expectant, and then, as I say, "Have a good night," there is some shifting of her facial features, some new resentment and understanding.

Back in my apartment, in bed beneath the covers, I imagine her naked on her knees. Her long hair is loose and swaying as her head bobs. But afterward, as I roll away from the wet spot to go to sleep, I know I won't return to her restaurant.

*My favorite moment in all of Strauss's writing is the finale
from "Der Rosenkavalier,"* she writes. *His lush late Roman-
ticism mixed with dissonance makes it so evocative and thrilling, to the point that even though I've listened many times, it
still almost brings me to tears (okay, maybe not almost). This
version is a trio, all sung by women. Amazing, no?*

"Do you remember Alicia Thompson?" Mark asks. "My
year in high school, tennis player, smoking hot body."

"Wasn't she prom queen?"

"That's the one. So I ran into her yesterday in the elevator at the hospital. She was bringing her dad in for an
echo. Let's just say when it comes to looks, she peaked
early."

"Has she been in St. Louis all this time?"

"She's married to a dude from Nashville, and I think
they were there for a few years. Or Memphis? Anyway—
back when she and I were seniors, she used to date Joe
Streizman. Right after we graduate, they break up, and
at a party at Tina Hoffer's house, Alicia and I end up
alone in the basement. We've both been drinking, and
she's full-on plastered and very touchy-feely. We're sitting really close together on this couch while she tells
me about the breakup, all weepy and shit, then she leans
in and whispers right in my ear—well, this is the eternal
mystery—she whispers either 'Hug me' or 'Fuck me.'
No kidding, it sounded like 'Fug me.' Maybe *she* didn't
know what she was asking for. Obviously, I should have
just said 'What?' But here I am, seventeen years old, with

a rock-hard boner, and my logic is, if I hug her and she said, 'Fuck me,' I'll get another chance. But if she said 'Hug me' and I fuck her, I'm a rapist."

"I take it you hugged her."

Cheerfully, Mark says, "Biggest mistake of my life."

"When you guys were in the elevator yesterday, did you ask her which she'd said?"

"Sure, in front of her dad. Why not?" As we head south on Big Bend, he adds, "I want to be like the Clintons. I don't want to be like the Gores. I want to ball other women but stay married."

"Anyone in particular?"

"There's this girl butcher at Whole Foods with a bunch of crazy tattoos. What's that rule for how young is too young—it's half your age plus seven, right? So if she's, what, twenty-eight, we're good to go." He pauses, then says slowly, "I don't think she's twenty-eight."

That ostensible rule means Thérèse needs to be twenty-seven, which she also isn't. But Mark knows about neither Thérèse nor Bonnie, and in any case, I don't anticipate crossing paths with Thérèse again.

I say, "Aren't open marriages just a stopgap until divorce?"

"Oh, I don't want an open marriage." Mark looks at me with distaste. "Where's the fun in that?"

"You don't want Libby to be involved with other men?"

"Of course not," he says. "But even more than that, I don't want another domestic agreement, another fucking chore chart. I don't want to have a respectful dialogue about how we can both get our needs met."

Mark has been complaining about his marriage for a

couple years, during which time, as far as I know, he and Libby haven't gone to counseling, he hasn't cheated on her, and he's expressed his dissatisfaction to her barely, if at all. What he wants, it seems, is simply to vent, which is to say that perhaps he *has* been in counseling, with an unaccredited therapist, who happens to be me.

"Don't cheat on her," I say.

From me: *Do you know the story behind "Symphonie fantastique"? Berlioz said it's about a man going insane because of how in love he is with a woman. Which is so awesomely dark and dreary! The real/autobiographical version is that Berlioz fell in love with an actress and wrote the piece to attract her. She eventually heard it, she married him, and they were miserable together. So if it's symphony as love letter, maybe that letter would have been better off left unanswered?*

After waiting three days, I text Bonnie again: *You free?*

She usually responds right away, but this time, unprecedentedly, she doesn't respond at all. It is possible, of course, that she's traveling, or that she lost her phone, or that she's simply preoccupied.

Just to be sure, I wait another day and text once more: *Hope all is well.*

Again, there is silence. And it's not that I didn't know this eventuality was possible, not that I don't understand. It's not even that I care much that she's ghosted me; I just wouldn't have guessed it to be her method of choice.

My favorite Berlioz is "Harold in Italy"—the viola concerto he wrote for Paganini, but Paganini rejected it because the viola part was too easy and not flashy enough. Then after hearing it, Paganini changed his mind. In addition to telling a story, it has weird phrase lengths. (Maybe related to Berlioz being a big user of drugs?) My favorite part is the 2nd movement, "Marche des pèlerins" (March of the Pilgrims). The viola starts to play ponticello arpeggios over the walking bass and it's a series of chord changes with this special trance-like sound. The first time I went to Paris, I heard it in my head as I wandered around.

Mark is standing in the driveway when I arrive, his legs spread, his torso tilted right, his left arm extended over his head. "You're not gonna fuckin' believe it," he says. "Libby's preggers. Guess the old sperm have got some juice yet."

No! I think. But this is a visceral reaction, and selfish; it's not that I don't want another child for Mark and Libby or, for that matter, a niece or another nephew. "Amazing," I say aloud.

"Fourteen-year age gap between our oldest and youngest kids." Mark holds his hand up for me to high-five and says, "No joke, this is gonna be the baby that launches a thousand vasectomies."

"But you're happy?" By which, of course, I mean, *Is this the point where we both start pretending you haven't spent the last few years confiding your adulterous fantasies?*

"Children are so life-affirming!" Mark says. "That moment when you bring home a newborn from the hospital, all tiny and wrapped in a blanket. You think, Jesus, everyone in the world was once this young, floating on a tide of parental love and hope. That's before they turn into teenage assholes."

It's hard not to wonder if it's really babies Mark loves, or if it's more that he's sentimental for the last time there were babies in his house—for when he was younger and his marriage was fresher. I am not, however, enough of a jerk to ask.

I've been running in place, and when he joins me, we head east. He adds, "Besides, she's the one who'll have to get up for most of the night feedings."

I knew already; she told me, via email, two months ago.

She wrote, *So I'm pregnant. Not on purpose. Haven't told Mark (yes, it's his, in case it seems like I'm implying otherwise—not physically possible that it WOULDN'T be). Anyway, if I get through the first trimester (and it's very plausible I won't, given my age) you and I should stop emailing. FYI.*

Wow, I replied. *Congratulations?*

A part of me always wanted a third, she wrote, *but I didn't expect it to happen at this late date. You think he'll be excited or freaked out?*

You'd know better than I would, I wrote back.

I wouldn't be so sure, she replied.

This was the first email about something other than music I'd received from her in ten months. In the beginning, many emails were about other things, though music was their point of origin. I'd been at their house for a

Sunday dinner, and Bach's Brandenburg Concerto no. 5 had been playing from a kitchen speaker as Libby pulled lasagna from the oven, I dressed the salad, and Finn set the table. I said, "I've always loved this piece," and Libby said, "Did you know it's the first-ever keyboard concerto?" I shook my head, and she said, "Because there were no pianos back then, just harpsichords." Then, seamlessly, she turned and said, "Finn, tell Dad and Noah to come in for dinner."

She emailed me the next afternoon, with a link to a version conducted by Claudio Abbado (*How great is the harpsichord cadenza in the first movement?*), and I emailed back concurring and adding that I hadn't realized she was such a classical music buff, to which she replied that she'd played viola from the age of seven to eighteen, that for years, her dream had been to attend Juilliard but that by the time she was in high school and entering competitions, it was clear she didn't have the talent, and she applied only to liberal arts colleges, not music schools. *You contain multitudes!* I wrote. *Good to know I better not try any classical music mansplaining.* In the following five days, during which, as usual, I ran with Mark twice, didn't lay eyes on Libby, and didn't discuss her with Mark, my sister-in-law told me over email that for her sixth-grade living biography, she had been Bach, that she'd never enrolled either of her sons in music lessons because she'd ended up so conflicted about her own but now she wondered if she'd made a mistake, and that the other day she hadn't been able to remember the word *Q-tip* and feared it was the first sign of early dementia; I told her that every year from third to seventh grade, I'd dressed as a so-called hobo for Halloween, that in grade school I had wanted to play the trumpet, but my mother had said I could either play soccer or take trumpet lessons but not both and I'd worried Mark would think I was lame if I opted for an instrument, and that sometimes descending stairs, I felt an intense, fleeting pain in my left knee that probably meant I wouldn't be able to keep running indefinitely, but for now I'd decided not to do anything about it. Somehow this morphed into Libby describing the school meeting she'd just left, at which a colleague of hers had not only fallen asleep but begun snoring audibly, and how Libby would definitely have awakened him if she'd been sitting closer, but she was fifteen feet away and unsure of whether the very act of standing and approaching him was more disruptive than the snoring, and then the meeting ended before she could decide. I told her about a client from years before who always removed both his shoes and his socks when he came to my office, without comment, as if this were normal, and she told me how when Noah was in first grade, she was the mom in charge of buying pumpkins for the kids at Halloween, and the pumpkins she got from a farm over the Illinois border were so dirty she had to give all fifty of them a bath. She wrote, *Does this affirm your choice not to reproduce? :)* We exchanged these emails at all hours of the day, into the evening, and that weekend, on both Friday and Saturday, we sent about fifteen each—we were debating what the best 1980s movie was, in terms of both quality and being most quintessentially eighties-ish—and at eleven-fifteen on Saturday night, she wrote, *I'm falling asleep so night night William.* Where was my brother at that moment? In bed beside her? In another part of the house? Was she in bed? Honestly, at the time, I didn't wonder. Less than twenty-four hours later, when I went to their house for Sunday dinner, Libby and I didn't discuss the emails, and after I was back home, at nine-thirty P.M., she wrote, *We can't do this anymore.*

I was genuinely surprised, and wrote back, *Why? Are you serious?*

Before I could confirm that I was, another message from her arrived: *Because I'm married to your brother.*

I considered not responding until the morning; I wanted a chance to collect my thoughts. But it occurred to me that she might interpret my silence as hurt feelings. *Libby, you're a wonderful person,* I wrote. *I adore you. But there's nothing remotely romantic about any of this.*

She didn't reply for forty-five minutes, which made me wonder if instead I'd hurt her feelings. Her response when it came: *If that's really what you think, I envy your ability to delude yourself.*

For the following week, we didn't communicate. It would be a lie to say I didn't miss her emails, to deny how quickly I'd embraced the existence of another consciousness with whom to exchange observations and experiences. And it would be a lie to claim I didn't feel some inner turmoil. But it wasn't the jilted person's turmoil; it was the uneasiness that accompanies a misunderstanding.

On Sunday, I went to dinner at their house with trepidation, and I suspect Libby and I were both straining to behave normally, which mostly took the form of avoiding each other; Finn and I played about thirty rounds of Horse in the driveway.

That Wednesday morning at ten o'clock, an email arrived, again sans greeting or sign-off. *I've thought about it and I think you were right and I was wrong and it's fine for us to email but let's keep it confined to music, nothing else. Driving to work this morning, I heard Górecki's Symphony no. 3. Do you know that one? So beautiful and devastating.*

I never explicitly agreed to her terms; I simply complied with them. We exchanged four or five emails a day for two days; then she wrote, *One more stipulation: We should only do this once a day. I'll email you between 8 a.m. and noon. You email me back between noon and four. No weekends.*

OK, I wrote.

This time, it lasted nearly a year, with neither of us deviating from the schedule, including when she, Mark, and the kids went to Aruba for Thanksgiving with her extended family. And it wasn't that I hadn't known there were certain gaps in my life; it was that I wouldn't have expected the gaps to be filled by receiving and writing one email per day about classical music, or that confining the topic didn't actually feel that different from the brief stretch when we'd been telling anecdotes; in some encoded, albeit not erotic, way, confining the topic felt *more* personal. I'd still found another consciousness; I still could experience the anticipation and satisfaction of contact, the mental absorption of composing a response in my head before sending it. Being in touch with her offered a cushioning to my days, an antidote to the tedium and indignity of being a person, the lack of accountability of my adulthood; it gave me stamina with Bonnie and willpower with Thérèse. I thought I'd achieved an equilibrium—one so eccentric as to be incomprehensible to most married suburban couples but, for me, one that could last. It felt sustainable in a way none of my relationships with girlfriends ever had.

I hear Mark told you, her message reads. *Or "told" you. Since I've made it through the first trimester, we need to stop. I know I don't have a ton of credibility on this front, but I mean it this time. I'm tempted to say something like Take care of yourself, as if I'm writing in your high school yearbook, when obviously we're* not *saying goodbye for real, just goodbye to this version of things.*

It's eleven A.M., but if the correspondence is ending anyway, I doubt that I need to wait until noon to reply. *Of course I'll respect your wishes,* I write, *but are you sure? At the risk of stating the obvious, we could tell Mark we enjoy emailing each other about classical music, and I think he'd be OK with it.*

She writes back, *Are you kidding? He'd be okay with it only insofar as he could mock us both.*

And then: *And it wouldn't be fun if he knew about it. ESPECIALLY if he was okay with it.*

And then: *When I said last year it was fine for us to keep emailing, I didn't mean it. To put it in legal terms for you, I was giving you the plausible deniability you seemed to need. Sure, marriages come in all shapes and sizes, but if one person is getting close to someone else, either both parts of the couple have to know and be on board or else it's a betrayal. Or, to use another legal term, a lie of omission.*

And finally: *The reason I pretended to think it was kosher when I didn't was that it had become too hard to get through the day without hearing from you. And the reason I restricted the times we emailed each other was that I was waiting all the time to hear back, which was unfair to my family and a fucked-up way to live. It's not that I actually*

WANT *to stop now, but there's too much at stake with a new baby. Mark and I need to be on the same team.*

It is physically difficult to read these sentences—not for their conclusion but for what comes before, their implicit rebuke, her distress. I have tried throughout my life to avoid upsetting women, yet I have done so repeatedly.

I consider being blunter than I ever have before, blunt in a way I'd convinced myself was unnecessary with the sister-in-law I've known for over twenty years. I could write, *I'm wired differently from most people. Call it my neurochemistry or call it my heart, but it doesn't work like yours. It doesn't feel what yours feels. My life would have been vastly easier if it did.*

If I express these sentiments, I know, because I've been through it before, that two outcomes are possible. The first is that she won't believe me, will cling to the idea of our being in love, and will plan to be the woman who's different from earlier women. She will think she can cure me.

The second outcome is that she *will* believe me. She might initially call me names—I've been accused of being a Tin Man, of possessing a Frankenheart, of having a condition found in the *Diagnostic and Statistical Manual of Mental Disorders*—but in the end what she'll feel is pity.

I do not want to be cured by her, and I do not want her pity.

I don't know what to say, yet it seems cruel to keep her waiting when she has made herself vulnerable. Thus I type, *Neither "plausible deniability" nor "lie of omission" is really a legal term. They're more like movie or TV versions of the law.*

Then I scroll through old messages, reread the one she wrote about Mozart's *Sinfonia Concertante in E-flat Major for Violin, Viola and Orchestra,* and listen to the piece in its entirety, while working on a brief. No message from her has arrived by the time the music concludes, but one comes in a minute later: *Take care of yourself, William.*

It's early March now, meaning the sun is rising when I reach their house; the eastern sky is pale blue and tangerine. Mark is stretching in the driveway again, and when he catches sight of me, he says, "Guillermo, my man. Salutations."

"You're in a good mood."

"Why wouldn't I be?" He lifts his chin and nods it once toward the master bathroom window, which is above the front door. "Look at that," he says. "Queen of my heart, vessel of my progeny."

Indeed, Libby is visible through the window; she's standing with her back to us, wearing a pink T-shirt. Is she about to sit on the toilet or did she just finish? Oh, our private habits, our private selves—how strange we all are, how full of feelings and essentially alone.

Mark wolf-whistles. If it's an inconsiderate thing to do to the neighbors at this hour of the morning, it works; Libby turns and looks out the window.

"Hey, sweetie," Mark says. Though I doubt she can hear him—he's speaking at a normal conversational volume— she waves. But she is too far away for me to discern the expression on her face.

A Regular Couple

After dinner, on the first night of our honeymoon, Jason and I were sitting in the hotel bar playing cribbage when, from thirty or forty feet away, I made eye contact with a woman who looked exactly like Ashley Frye. Jason was dealing the cards—our travel version of cribbage comes in a zippered case with a miniature plastic board that unfolds and tiny pegs, and although the dorkiness of it makes me slightly self-conscious, it doesn't make me self-conscious enough not to break it out—and I said, "There's someone over there who's identical to a bitchy girl I went to high school with."

Jason glanced over his shoulder. "Who?"

"The blonde by the fireplace, but I'm sure it's not her." It was 2008, we were at the fanciest resort in a fancy western town, and I had graduated from high school in Cleveland in 1992. It's not that the area where I grew up wasn't nice; it was a suburb inhabited by families with dads who worked in law or finance, and even though my high school was public, it was cushier than a lot of private schools. But the hotel where Jason and I were staying was mostly a ski resort, and this was in July. Running into Ashley Frye in the off-season would have been odd, and besides, the woman who looked like her was with a man who was probably fifteen years older, a little heavy, and generally too fatigued-seeming and unremarkable to be attached to Ashley Frye. "That girl was the queen of my high school," I said.

"You were close friends, I assume?" Jason was smiling. He knows what I was like as a teenager—flat-chested and stringy-haired, the daughter not of a banker but of a science teacher—and my husband appears to find it endearing, this vision of me as awkward and clueless, I think because he considers me so confident and strong-willed now. More than once, he's said, "You have bigger balls than I do." If this is a compliment, obviously it's not one that most women hope to receive from their husbands.

I put down a three of spades, then Jason played the three of hearts and said, "Six for a pair."

"Maggie?"

The Ashley Frye look-alike was standing beside our table, the older man slightly behind her. She laid her palm against her chest. "Maggie, it's Ashley from Clarke High." Her hair was a more honeyed blond than it had been when we were teenagers—it looked expensively dyed—and she had the same ski-jump nose and wide green eyes. She also had crow's-feet, lines at the corners of her lips, and a certain haggard leanness through her face. She was definitely still pretty, but not like she'd been in high school; that pretty had seemed to guarantee whatever life she'd wanted, whatever boy, whereas the pretty she was now was that of a well-groomed, mid-level

professional—a pharmaceutical rep, perhaps. Nevertheless, I felt an old, visceral insecurity that manifested itself
in an impulse to cover up our cribbage game with my
hands. This was when Ashley said, "I'm sure you don't
remember me, but I just said to my husband—this is my
husband, Ed—I said, 'Maggie will have no idea who I
am, but I have to go over anyway.' I know everyone must
tell you this, but whenever we see you on TV, I'm like, 'I
totally know her!' That's what I say, right, Ed?" She
turned back to me. "Ed and I just got married. We're on
our honeymoon."

I hesitated—partly because I wasn't sure what to make
of her effusiveness and partly because, although Ashley
didn't seem aware of it, I actually hadn't appeared on
television in nearly two years—and Jason said, "What do
you know? We're on our honeymoon, too."

Ashley's mouth fell open with delight. "What are the
chances?" she said. "When Ed and I made our reserva-
tions, I thought, This is such a weird time to come that I
bet the whole resort will be a ghost town." I had imagined the same, and been surprised when we checked in to
find the lobby abuzz. Ashley extended her hand to Jason.
"Ashley Horsford," she said. Glancing at me, she added,
"That's what I go by now. Still getting used to the sound
of it!"

Jason introduced himself and half-stood to shake
her hand, then Ed's, and I shook Ed's, too. He made
a one-syllable noise of acknowledgment, possibly something that wasn't an actual word. *This* was the husband
of Ashley Frye? He was okay, not ugly, but there was
nothing about him that made me remotely jealous. He
was like a generic man I'd end up next to on the flight

from O'Hare to LaGuardia, hardly notice as I sat down, never really look at as I worked on my laptop during the flight, and not recognize by the time we reached the baggage claim. His face was broad and ruddy, and he was balding, with a few brown locks brushed back from his forehead and fuller hair along the sides. He wasn't fat, but he had that paunch you sometimes see on guys who were high school athletes and have spent the decade or two since then working a sedentary job and drinking a steady stream of alcohol. Another part of what made him seem older was that he was wearing a blue-and-white-striped button-down shirt and a blazer, while Jason had on a long-sleeved T-shirt. We hadn't eaten dinner at the resort but, instead, had walked to a pizza place in town, about three-quarters of a mile away, and by the time we walked back, the temperature had fallen below sixty degrees.

"When did you guys get here?" Ashley asked.

"Just today," I said.

"Oh, you'll love it. We got here— Ed, what day was it? I'm already losing track."

"Sunday," Ed said.

"Right, of course, we're staying Sunday to Sunday. How stressful is it having your whole wedding and then you're supposed to jump on a plane the next morning? We almost missed our flight."

"Jason and I actually got married four months ago," I said. I felt a sort of hierarchical confusion about how to act toward Ashley, how nice or standoffish to be. If she hadn't started gushing so quickly, I'm sure I'd have been willing to take the deferential role—old habits die hard—but clearly I now had the opportunity to present an aloof version of myself she'd never met. My confusion was different from the usual confusion I felt when approached in public, which almost never happened anymore. Back when it had happened, I couldn't be sure if the person was going to praise or attack me. The biggest clues, I'd realized over time, were age and gender: My peers, both male and female, tended to be like Ashley in thinking it was cool that they'd seen me on TV, while women my mother's age were likelier to scold me, taking me to task for betraying feminism. The first time this had ever happened was at the gym near my office in downtown Chicago; it was a middle-aged woman, and I ended up talking to her for half an hour by the elliptical machines, defending myself—I went on a monologue about due process, and by the end of the conversation, I was very flushed, even though I hadn't yet started exercising—but I quickly realized that trying to explain my job, or the American legal system, served little purpose. Within a few weeks of that gym encounter, I stopped saying anything more to my critics than "Obviously, you're entitled to your opinion." Then I'd walk away.

"Be sure to take the cable car up Mount Majesty," Ashley was saying. "That was our favorite thing so far, right, Ed? Oh, and we're hiking to Moose Lake tomorrow, which is supposed to be amazing."

Oh, Jesus, I thought, because that was what Jason and I had been planning, too. Then I thought we could easily go to Moose Lake on a different day, and then I heard Jason say, "We're going there tomorrow, too. It's clearly the place to be." I knew that if I made eye contact with him, it would be to glare, so instead I looked at Ashley.

"Well, I don't know what time you're taking off," she

said, "but if you wanted to, we could all . . ." She giggled a little, and it was such a tentative sound that I almost felt sorry for her. But even then I was conscious of feeling sorry not for Ashley Frye but for Ashley Horsford. She added, "I mean, probably you guys want alone time, since you just arrived. . . ."

There was a momentary silence—Jason was deferring to me, at least now that he'd set this situation in motion—and because I couldn't deal with the awkwardness of declining, I said, "Why don't we touch base in the morning?"

"Oh, this'll be so fun!" Ashley exclaimed. "We're in Room 412. What number are you?"

"We're in one of the cabins." I turned back to Jason. "It's called Juniper, right?"

I saw Ashley registering this information—the rooms cost $400 a night, and the cabins cost $800—but all she said was "Great, then. We'll call you tomorrow." She stepped forward, setting her hand on my arm. "And really, Maggie, I know this sounds corny, but I'm so impressed by your success. I always knew you'd go far." Her last comment was such an enormous lie that I longed for the courage to dismiss it, right there and to her face, for the bullshit it was. The reality, however, is that my balls aren't as big as my husband imagines, and I simply said "Thanks."

I waited until Ashley and Ed had left the bar before saying to Jason, "Why did you do that?"

"Man, was she fawning over you." He shook his head.

"That's what you want to listen to all day tomorrow?"

Jason laughed. "Maybe she got it out of her system."

"I don't understand why you invited them to join us right after I told you I never liked her."

"She suggested it, and *you* agreed to it, not me. Relax, Magpie." Jason himself seemed perfectly relaxed—he pretty much always does, which is one of his best qualities, except when it's infuriating.

"I don't think you get it. It's not like she's this annoying but harmless person. She's kind of evil."

At this, Jason really laughed, and I said, "I'm not kidding. She once—" I hadn't thought about this for years. Even though I wasn't cool in high school, I'm not haunted by it. I've lived in Chicago since college, I go back to Cleveland for a couple days at Thanksgiving or Christmas, and that's it. My sister and I revert to our much younger selves, we bake chocolate-chip cookies and order pizza and watch *The Cutting Edge* or the *Anne of Green Gables* miniseries from the eighties, while Jason and my dad play basketball in the driveway. I never call anyone from my past—I've never gone to a high school reunion, never tried to, like, *redeem* myself in some public setting, among the people I once knew.

"Ashley wasn't in my grade," I said. "She was a year younger. And when she started as a freshman, right away, she got a lot of attention. She was sort of crowned the official prettiest freshman. And in my class was this girl who was our year's equivalent of Ashley, Jenny Josephson, and Jenny Josephson went out with a guy named Bobby, who—"

"Wait," Jason interrupted. "Am I supposed to pretend I'm actually following this?"

"I think you're up to the challenge," I said. "Early in our sophomore year, which was Ashley's freshman year, rumors started that Bobby was going to dump Jenny Josephson for Ashley. I didn't believe it because, you know,

Jenny and Bobby were our super-couple. But it took on this tone of inevitability, like someone somewhere had decided that Ashley was even hotter than Jenny, and so Bobby had no choice but to pursue her. He was the quarterback—did I mention that?"

"Of course he was," Jason said.

"So Ashley and Bobby become a couple, and Jenny is completely traumatized. She didn't come to school for a week, and I heard she'd started cutting herself. This was in 1989, and I barely even knew what cutting was. Ashley and Bobby are dating, and then at a party a few weeks later—needless to say, I wasn't there—Ashley cheats on him with some other football player, so she and Bobby break up, Bobby and Jenny Josephson get back together, and Ashley starts going out with the other football player. I don't even think she'd ever really liked Bobby. It had just been some big ego trip, but she'd practically destroyed Jenny Josephson in the process."

"Why was it Ashley's fault?" Jason said. "Wasn't Bobby equally responsible?"

"Bobby was in the wrong, too," I said. "But Ashley shouldn't have poached another girl's boyfriend."

Jason raised his eyebrows, which was supposed to show that he was restraining himself from remarking, as he does on a regular basis, that I'm too hard on my own gender. I strongly disagree with this assessment and consider myself an equal-opportunity faultfinder.

"Anyway, none of that is the reason I don't like her," I said. "Ashley and I were both on the volleyball team, and once we were the last ones leaving the locker room before practice. We weren't talking. I was just standing by my locker, and she came over and said, 'Will you tie my shoe?' She put her foot on my thigh—I was wearing shorts, so the sole of her shoe was pressed against my skin—and I tied it, and she kind of smirked and walked out of the locker room. This was stupid of me, but when she'd asked, I'd assumed she'd injured herself and that's why she couldn't tie her own shoe—because otherwise, why would you ask someone to do it for you? But I watched her at practice, and she obviously wasn't injured at all, and I realized she'd just been trying to, like, degrade me for her own amusement. That was the most obnoxious part, the pathological part. It would have been meaner but less weird if she'd had an audience and was trying to impress them by humiliating me. But she was just getting her jollies by herself."

"Strange." Jason's tone was calm.

"That's your only reaction?"

"What do you want me to say? She doesn't seem like that person anymore. Obviously, if anything, she's intimidated by you. But I couldn't care less, so let's blow them off."

"We'll keep running into them until they leave."

"Who cares, if she's this person you don't like and never plan to see again?"

"I don't want to spend the next forty-eight hours hiding from her."

"Do you want to switch hotels?"

I scrutinized Jason's face. "Are you joking?"

"This is our honeymoon," he said. "You're supposed to enjoy yourself."

I was quiet before saying, "How old do you think her husband is?"

"Forty, maybe."

"What do you think his job is?"

"Gynecologist."

"Seriously."

"How should I know? I-banking or something."

"Do you think Ashley's hot?" I asked.

Jason pondered the question for a few seconds. "She's hot, but in a cheesy way. You know, what she looks like is a pharmaceutical rep."

I felt so filled with love for him in that moment that, honestly, I almost teared up.

"Magpie," he said. When our eyes met, he gestured at the table, where I'd set my cards down at Ashley's approach. "It's your turn."

The way it came to pass that Ashley saw me on TV, the way I came to be scolded by strangers for betraying feminism, is that I entered law school right after getting my BA; worked very, very hard; became editor of the law review; was offered a job as an associate at Corster, Lemp, Shreiberg, and Levine, the civil-litigation and criminal-defense firm in Chicago where I'd spent the summers interning; continued to work very, very hard; and in 2005, after seven years, became the youngest person in the firm's history, male or female, to make partner. Eight months later, while he was in Chicago to receive an award from a national organization dedicated to mentoring at-risk youth, Billy Kendall, a linebacker for the Carolina Panthers, invited a cocktail waitress back to his room after an evening of flirting at the bar in the lobby of the Sofitel and proceeded to either rape her (her version) or to have consensual sex with her (his version). Kendall hired Corster, Lemp, Shreiberg, and Levine to represent him, and how could it hurt the defense if one of Kendall's lawyers was not only a woman but a woman about the same age as his accuser?

I'm not under any illusions; I realize the fact that I was the second seat for the trial, and that I was the one who cross-examined the cocktail waitress, wasn't entirely due to my legal prowess, but I was not, as I know cynics suspected, just loitering around the counsel table, buffing my nails. Indeed, I prepared more rigorously than I'd ever prepared for any other trial—researching similar cases, poring over the police reports and witness statements, drafting and redrafting my cross-examination. Still, it's indisputable that if not for my age and gender, I wouldn't have been picked to appear on the cable-news shows during the three-week trial. I appeared mostly via satellite, when—I had never realized this was how TV worked—I'd be in a television studio in Chicago, looking at a blank screen and trying to seem engaged while the voice of the show's host in New York or Atlanta was piped into my ear. I'd met with a media coach for four hours before my television debut, at Billy Kendall's expense—in fact, probably unbeknownst to him, Kendall was not only paying for the coach but also paying me for the hours I spent with the coach—and the guy had recommended, as a way of not looking zoned out when I wasn't the one talking, that I pretend the blank screen was a beloved elderly relative and that I smile in an open and encouraging way, but not to excess. The week after Billy Kendall was acquitted, I flew to New York for a fifteen-minute sit-down interview—an eternity in television time—with the host of a broadcast evening-news program. I actually found all the TV stuff stressful, but people who knew me, including my family, got a kick out of it, even if what I was on TV for was defending a man accused of rape.

The one person consistently unimpressed by my role in the trial was Jason, whom I'd been dating for a little less than a year and who was still in law school, spending the summer interning for an eight-person nonprofit that specialized in immigration services. After my first interview on national television, when I'd called Jason as I rode home from the local studio in a cab, I expressed surprise that the news anchor hadn't seemed to know the difference between civil and criminal trials—he had kept referring to "the plaintiff's side"—and Jason said, " 'Television is a medium because it's neither rare nor well-done.' Isn't that how that saying goes?"

Sitting in the back of the cab, I thought, *Really? I was just on CNN and that's your reaction?* Then again, I had been disparaging first, and he had merely concurred.

I'd met Jason shortly after I made partner but before I started working on the Kendall case. A law school professor, a woman I consider my mentor, invited me to speak to her Criminal Procedure class, and Jason was a student, a 2L. He was actually a year older than I was but had spent the decade after college working in Honduras and El Salvador for an American aid organization, as I learned at the reception afterward when he came up to me, made small talk, then asked for my email address. Two days later, he emailed to ask if I wanted to meet for a drink. I was skeptical at first because Jason was not only significantly better-looking than my previous boyfriends but also a more attractive man than I am a woman, which, if you start paying attention, is a highly unusual dynamic. (I've concluded that there are more attractive women than men in the world, so the numbers work in men's favor.) At first I couldn't believe that this smart, even-keeled guy with curly brown hair and bright blue eyes was into me, and I still mostly feel this way—Jason is indeed smart and even-keeled, with curly brown hair and bright blue eyes—but it also strikes me, in retrospect, that if a young male partner from a law firm had come to talk to my Criminal Procedure class when I was a student, I would never have had the confidence to ask him out; I'd have asked him for a job, possibly, but not for a date.

Jason and I hadn't been one of those couples that immediately become inseparable. I didn't have time to see him more than once or twice a week, because I routinely worked until ten o'clock. After that first time we had drinks, Jason called to see if I wanted to get dinner—dinner on a Saturday night, a full-on date of the sort I'd been on only a handful of times, even though I was then thirty-one—and afterward we went to watch a movie at his apartment and I fell asleep ten minutes in. We hadn't kissed yet except for a brief peck after the first date. Jason told me later that my falling asleep plus my general unavailability made him doubt that I liked him, and it's occurred to me that he kept pursuing me for that very reason.

Because honestly, to this day, I don't know what made him interested in me. It's not that I hate myself, at least not most of the time—it's just that it wouldn't have been difficult for Jason to find a woman who was prettier, or more of a fighter for the underdog, or both. The one time I asked him about it, and I tried to ask as casually, as unpathetically, as possible, given that it's an inherently pathetic question, he said, "Because you had your act together." I think he was referring less to my career than to my not being anorexic or flat-out insane, in contrast to his previous girlfriends; one of them had literally weighed all her meals on a postage scale. Then he added, grinning, "And because you were a good lay." I made a face when he said this, and he said, "What? That's the ultimate compliment!"

I wonder, of course—it's my deepest secret, and would likely be guessable to even a distant acquaintance—if Jason married me for my money. Not only for my money, but if my income nudged me into some category of desirability I might not otherwise have attained. Jason is for the little guy, yes, but he has quietly expensive taste. He spends more on clothes than I do—on Italian leather loafers or simple crewneck sweaters that, lo and behold, are cashmere—and he enjoys a good steak and a nice cocktail. Whereas my own enjoyment of these things is always accompanied by uneasiness—I still can't order a thirty-dollar entrée without thinking, Holy shit, thirty dollars for an entrée?

These days, I make twenty times what Jason does, and we spend money in a way he never could on just his salary, and in a way neither of our families did when we were growing up. We'll get a seventy-dollar bottle of wine with dinner at a restaurant on an ordinary Tuesday; we have a cleaning service that comes twice a week to the condo that I paid for in cash before we got married. And we almost willfully blew through money when planning our honeymoon. For months, we didn't make any deci-

sions about when or where we were going, and then one
night in late spring, Jason said, "Let's just hammer it out
before we never go at all," and so we ordered Thai food
and brought our laptops to the dining room table and
separately poked around websites for a destination and
hotels and flights. Mostly we wanted it to be easy—no
long flights, no intricate research required beforehand or
on our arrival—but Jason also thought that lying on a
beach for a week sounded boring, so we settled on coming out west. He was the one who found our hotel. At
our dining room table, he said, "They have these cool
little cabins."

I leaned over so I could see his computer screen and
said, "For eight hundred dollars a night?"

"What? We can afford it." Sometimes when we discussed finances, Jason's pronouns made my skin prickle—
how casually he'd say *we* instead of *you*. Also, there was
the fact that if he were the one earning more money, as
in a traditional couple, there were certain ways I'd probably defer to him, accommodations I'd make that he
seemed either unconcerned with or unaware of: He did
significantly less of the cooking, rarely sorted the mail,
and never made our bed. He would do any of these
things if I asked, but he didn't do them, as if they didn't
need doing, as long as I didn't ask. We hadn't signed a
prenup because, against my better judgment and legal
training, I'd pretended I found it persuasive—I'd pretended I wasn't afraid he'd change his mind about me—
when he said, "So not only do you think we'll end up
divorced but you think I'll try to screw you over when we
do?" We kept our savings accounts separate, but you
don't need a law degree to know that that's legally mean-

ingless. As a wedding present, I paid off his student loans. I'd wondered ahead of time if he'd let me, but declining didn't seem to occur to him. He'd said, "Really? Thanks." If I'd expected him to gasp, tear up, or otherwise express touched astonishment, I'd mistaken him for someone else.

He'd proposed to me on New Year's Eve 2007, which we had spent at home, watching *National Lampoon's Vacation* and drinking champagne. It wasn't even eleven P.M., as the credits rolled, when he turned and said, "There's something I was thinking about during the movie. I was thinking we should get married." I know this isn't a particularly romantic proposal, but I was so happy that I didn't realize there was no ring.

He was the one who said, a few minutes later, that together we should select something without diamonds.

"Because of the whole blood-diamond thing?" I asked.

"There's that," he said. "But mostly I just think they're tacky and ostentatious."

"But you're fine spending shitloads of money in ways other people can't see?"

He smiled. "Pretty much."

"Jason, engagement rings have diamonds in them. It's the norm."

"Yeah, because 1940s jewelers brainwashed generations of American women."

"Is this about . . ." I hesitated, searching for a diplomatic way to put it. "The expense?"

He seemed more amused than offended. "I'm not indigent. You really can't believe that I just think diamonds are ugly?"

"It seems awfully convenient."

He shrugged. "I'm happy to get you a ring with some other kind of stone."

I hadn't previously given the matter much thought, but not having a diamond engagement ring suddenly seemed like being fake-engaged—being "engaged." Months before he'd proposed, we'd agreed that if we got married, it would be at the courthouse, with only our families present, and it wasn't as if I was going to wear a big white dress. Was wanting this one token of the establishment all that materialistic? I said, "What if I say I really want a diamond ring?"

Still amiable, still unruffled, Jason said, "Then you should buy one for yourself."

And then—I'm not sure which of us was calling the other's bluff—I did. Three days later, I walked into the Tiffany's on Michigan Avenue and walked out an hour later with a $38,000 cushion-cut ring that I'd charged to my Platinum Amex. This was a sum I'd never have let Jason spend, or spent on myself, if I weren't trying to make a point. And, of course, the ring didn't fit right—it was too big, but I took it anyway, figuring I'd get it sized later. Outside the door of our condo, I put the ring on, and inside, when I held out my left hand to Jason, he said, "Whatever floats your boat, Magpie," and I burst into tears. He ended up putting his arm around my shoulders as we sat on the couch and I sobbed and said, "I don't understand why we can't just be a regular couple."

"What does that even mean?" he asked.

The next day, over dinner, he gave me a pair of fairtrade malachite earrings from India. Because I am either needy or an asshole or both, I later went to the store they'd come from to see how much they cost. They were seventy-four dollars.

By the time we were half an hour past the trailhead leading to Moose Lake, Jason and Ed were twenty yards ahead of Ashley and me. Sometimes I could hear the men's voices but not their words, and I wondered what they were discussing. Ashley had been telling me about her job, which was in the marketing department of a gas company in Stamford, Connecticut; Ed worked as a developer in commercial construction. "I'm about to switch gears, though," she said. "I'm starting my own PR firm, me and this other girl."

"Cool," I said.

The trail was narrow, and Ashley was walking in front of me. Over her shoulder, she said, "I have this moron for a boss, and it's like, Why should I do all the work and he gets all the credit?" Below her daypack, I could see her little butt, encased in jogging shorts, and her tan, shapely legs, which ended in gray wool socks and hiking boots. Even though we were surrounded by birch trees and wildflowers and distant snow-peaked mountains, my attention was on Ashley—I detested myself for this, and I also couldn't help it.

"You know the number one thing people say when I tell them I'm starting a business?" she continued. "They're like, 'But don't you want kids? You're not getting any younger!'"

"There's definitely a double standard," I said.

"Not that I don't want kids ever," she said. "But why rush? Do you guys want children?"

"Maybe," I said. The real answer was very likely not, but I had learned from experience that revealing the truth would elicit a torrent of protests about the cuteness of tiny toes and fingers, the unique meaning imbued by parenthood. None of which I doubted, but I was fine not experiencing the toes, fingers, or unique meaning first-hand. To be a senior partner at Corster, I couldn't work less than I already did—I usually billed upwards of two hundred hours a month—and I didn't see the point of enduring pregnancy and childbirth and then hiring someone else to raise my kid while I was racked with guilt. Jason was more on the fence. He'd said he could go either way, which made it seem like deciding whether to sit at a booth or a table in a restaurant, but I didn't want to press the point in case he came down on the pro-kid side.

Ashley said, "Everyone tries to scare you, like, *tick, tick, tick,* but two of the women in my office got pregnant when they were forty."

"You're younger than I am, aren't you?" I said. "Weren't you the year behind me in school?"

"Oh, that's right." Ashley laughed. "It's funny because I remember us as classmates, but I must just be thinking of volleyball."

Behind her on the trail, I couldn't help sneering. That she "remembered us" in any particular way seemed ludicrous, given that we'd hardly spoken besides the day in the locker room when she'd asked me to tie her shoe.

We'd ridden together in the volleyball van countless times, but I had always sat in the first row, and she, Suzanne Green, and Tina Millioti had sat in the back. Once, after we lost to a team at a school on the West Side, when we were still in the parking lot outside their gym, Ashley, Suzanne, and Tina had begun chanting, "That's all right, that's okay, you're gonna work for us someday!" Our coach had been so mad that when we stopped for dinner at McDonald's, she made them stay in the van.

"Wasn't high school miserable?" Ashley said then, and I wondered if I'd heard her correctly, or even, perhaps, if she was making fun of me.

Neutrally, I said, "How so?"

"We were all so insecure, right? It was like this seething mass of hormones and nervousness."

I said, "You never seemed like a particularly nervous person."

She turned her head, smiling. "Yeah, well, I played it cool, but I threw up every morning before school for most of freshman year."

Was she serious? If so, this would have once been a fascinating tidbit, it would have forced me to reexamine my entire worldview, but what was I supposed to do with it now?

"So Jason's super-cute," Ashley said. "How'd you meet?"

"At law school." This response was true enough, and easier than going into detail. And I can't deny that I derived a certain pleasure from Ashley Frye—Ashley Horsford—affirming my husband's cuteness, but again, I kept my tone noncommittal. "What about you and Ed?"

"I roomed with his sister in college. I first met him when I was eighteen, but we didn't reconnect until Kate's wedding."

"Is Ed older or younger than his sister?" I tried to act as if the question had just occurred to me.

But Ashley sounded cheerful as she said, "Older— Ed's thirty-four, but he looks like an old man, doesn't he? And he acts like one, too. He gets all cranky if he can't take a dump at the same time every morning, or if I make him try anything new. He's never even had sushi."

Thirty-four? So Ed was my age exactly, and a year younger than Jason.

"He was really traditional about proposing, too," she said. "First I was dropping hints, then I was asking him straight up what the deal was, and finally I was like, 'Okay, you don't even have to do anything formal, but can we just say we're engaged?' He's like, 'Calm down, Ashley.' Turns out he wanted to ask my dad first."

Ashley, and not Ed, had been the one pushing for marriage? Shouldn't he have been pursuing her? Although I didn't find her appealing, I'd seen no evidence that he had more to offer. That morning, when we'd met in the lobby and walked to the parking lot, he'd said to Jason, "You catch that shitty pitching in the Rockies game last night?" and he hadn't initiated any other conversation during the half-hour drive to the Moose Lake trail.

"Your engagement ring is gorgeous, by the way," Ashley said. Apparently she'd taken note of it earlier, because she didn't turn around as she spoke.

"Thanks." I couldn't remember what hers looked like, so I didn't reciprocate the compliment. Instead, I stepped off the trail and peered toward our husbands, wondering if they'd pause so we could catch up.

Although Moose Lake turned out to be as beautiful as promised, a glassy blue expanse that showed the upside-down reflection of the mountain, I still felt distracted by our companions; Ashley's personality overrode the mountains and the water and the meadows of yellow and purple flowers. When we posed for pictures, Ashley put her arm around me, so I reluctantly put my arm around her. Would she post this on Facebook? Before we hiked back, we sat by the lake and ate sandwiches we'd picked up at a bakery on the way out of town. In the car, as soon as I could get a signal, I checked my BlackBerry.

Back at the resort, before we parted ways, Ed said to Jason, "Call me after dinner," and Jason said, "Will do."

"Oh, fun," Ashley said. "Are we meeting up for a drink?"

Ugh, I thought.

"For cigars," Ed said. "Men only."

"Thanks a lot," Ashley said. "Not like it's our honeymoon or anything."

Jason and I looked at each other, and he said, "I'll be in touch, Ed."

As Jason and I walked out the rear exit of the lobby and toward the path leading to the cabins, Ashley called after me, "I say we crash boys' night, if only to punish them."

Once we were outside again, the late afternoon smelled clean and sweet and piney, and the sunlight was mellower than it had been during the hike. It wouldn't get dark until nine-thirty. I said, "Since when do you smoke cigars?"

"You don't know everything about me." Jason said it jokingly, like a child declaring, You're not the boss of me. As if this were an explanation, he added, "They're Cuban."

We got room service for dinner, and as we finished eating, Ashley called. She said, "Since the boys are being sexist about tonight, why don't you guys join us for dinner tomorrow? We made a reservation at Piquant, and they can change it to four."

Piquant was, I knew from reading the guidebook in our room, a swanky new restaurant in town. Because it didn't seem worth the effort of declining—if I did, she'd probably just initiate something else—I said, "Okay." Or maybe my willingness to accommodate her was the true measure of how tense Ashley still made me.

"Great!" she said. "The reservation's at eight. This is the last hurrah for us before it's back to the daily grind. Will you put Jason on? Ed wants to talk to him."

I heard Jason agree to meet Ed in twenty minutes on the patio outside the bar. When Jason hung up, I said, "I told her we'd have dinner with them tomorrow night and, yes, I know."

"You know what?" Jason laughed. "That you're a hypocrite or a pushover?"

"Would you rather be married to him or her?"

"I'd rather be married to you," Jason said.

"But if you had to pick?"

"I'd leave them both at the altar." Then he said, "Her,

because at least she has a personality. He's a fucking rock."

"Remind me why you're about to go hang out with him?"

"Didn't we already establish this?" Jason leaned in and kissed my forehead. "I'm using him for his cigars."

For dinner the next night, Ed drove again. The decor of the restaurant seemed self-conscious—tiny multicolored tiles on the walls of the dining room, a sink in the women's bathroom that was a long, flat piece of slate on which water pooled in ways I was pretty sure weren't intentional—and the food was mediocre. We finished five bottles of wine, all of which Ed selected, and we split the bill down the middle. (Jason threw in his credit card, which was always how we did it when we ate with other couples.) When we reemerged into the night, after eleven P.M., I was solidly drunk. As we turned off the main drag to walk toward where the car was parked, I had a vision of Ed slamming the SUV into a deer, or something more exotic—a moose or a black bear. Before we got to the car, though, Ashley cried out, "Oh, this is the local dive bar! We have to go in!" She'd already opened the oversized wooden door and gone inside. I was glad no actual locals seemed to have heard her.

Unlike our hotel, this was a place where smoking inside was definitely still allowed. Most of the tables were full, and the people looked less preppy than at the resort—they wore jeans and jean jackets and flannel shirts. Willie Nelson was playing on a jukebox in the corner, and, a few feet from it, Ashley found an empty booth.

After a waitress took our drink order, Ashley leaned across the table toward me—our husbands had started discussing baseball again—and said, "I'm so glad we got to spend this time together." I noticed a tiny black something—maybe only pepper—wedged next to her canine tooth. It didn't count as real food stuck in her teeth, it wasn't necessarily the kind of thing she herself would notice during a quick trip to the bathroom, but it seemed like some final, culminating piece of evidence, as if I still needed one, that her high school self no longer existed. *RIP, Ashley Frye,* I thought.

"My friend Cindy warned me that the secret of honeymoons no one tells you is that they're really boring and make you second-guess your whole marriage," she was saying. Even though I was sitting on the other side of the booth from her, her face was about three inches too close to mine; as she continued speaking, I realized she was trying to prevent her husband from overhearing, which was unnecessary, given the volume of the music. "There's been all this activity leading up to the wedding, then you get away from it and the two of you stare at each other and have nothing to say. So we ran into you and Jason just in time, huh?"

The theory didn't strike me as entirely wrong—more than once, I've thought that cribbage will probably do more in the long term for my marriage than sex—but I felt annoyed by Ashley's implication that we had mutually rescued each other. I gave her what I hoped was a cold smile.

Her face was still overly close to mine as she said, "Did you ever think in high school we'd become two old married ladies?"

"We're not that old," I said.

She laughed merrily. "We will be!" She was definitely as drunk as I was, if not more so.

"I need to use the bathroom." I stood abruptly, before she could decide to come along. So far, I'd been careful to stagger my bathroom visits, and even my outdoor pees on the hike, so they occurred separately from hers. I knew myself well enough to know I'd be unable to go with her nearby—another vestige of adolescence.

When I emerged, she was standing at the jukebox. "I'm trying to find good early-nineties songs," she said. "Remember 'Nothing Compares 2 U'? But that's kind of a downer." She kept pressing the button to turn the pages behind the glass, and I saw her select a song by Madonna.

Back at the table, our drinks had arrived. There was a group discussion of Chicago real estate, then Ashley said, "Jason, I just realized I don't even know what you do."

"Immigration lawyer," he said.

"Keeping them in or out?" Ed asked, and Jason said, "I work mostly on asylum cases."

I wasn't sure Ed or Ashley would know what this meant, but Ashley immediately said, "Oh, he's your conscience!"

Even in my drunkenness, I stiffened. "If you're referring to the Kendall case, it was decided by jurors, not lawyers," I said, and under the table, I felt Jason set his hand on my knee.

"But everyone knows the dude was guilty. He's a total thug!" The difference in the way Ashley said this and the way middle-aged feminists had said almost the same words was that Ashley's tone was upbeat; apparently, she thought Billy Kendall had raped the cocktail waitress, and she also didn't really care.

I said, "Kendall was acquitted because the prosecution didn't have sufficient evidence against him. As for Jason being my conscience, I'd say it's more like I'm his gravy train."

Jason removed his hand—I didn't look at him—and Ed said, "Dude, does she always bust your chops like that?"

I stood. "I'm walking back to the hotel. I need some air."

"Don't get mad just because I said Kendall's a thug." Ashley made a pouty face. "Jason, tell your wife she's being a spoilsport."

Without really making eye contact with me, Jason said, in an unfriendly tone, "You're walking?"

I strongly wanted him to go with me; I also knew that if I were him, I wouldn't. This was when I heard the beginning of "Vogue," that part where Madonna says in an aggressive voice, "Strike a pose."

Ashley exclaimed and jumped up from the table; she immediately began swaying her hips, her mouth open wide. Then she was tugging on my hand, dancing around me. I shook my head. She said, "But doesn't it take you back?" She'd begun making the moves from the video, holding her hands sideways above and below her face.

I said—I had to speak loudly, over the music—"Dance with your husband."

"Ed doesn't dance." She made a face. "You guys are lame." She turned then, and very quickly—seamlessly— she grabbed Jason's hands, and he let her pull him up and toward the jukebox. It wasn't as if there was a dance floor, or as if anyone else was dancing, but he followed her lead. This is the thing: Jason is a good dancer. He's a good dancer, and he likes dancing, and he ended up with a woman whose dancing is restricted to the electric slide at family weddings. I glanced at Ed and said, "I guess it's clear who the introverts and extroverts are."

Ed didn't respond, and I wondered for the first time if he knew something I didn't. For all I disdained her, I'd expended a lot of energy on Ashley in the past few days. But Ed didn't seem to make an effort for anyone.

A minute passed, and although the smart thing to do would have been to follow Ed's example and shut up, I couldn't, for the same reason I couldn't leave the bar while Ashley and Jason were still dancing. If one of them looked over, which they weren't doing, I wanted them to see us talking.

"Ashley mentioned she's starting her own business," I said. "A PR company, right?"

He took a sip of scotch and said, "Not gonna happen."

"What do you mean?"

"The economy's about to crater. Nobody'll be hiring an unproven quantity." I'm embarrassed to admit that this was the first I'd heard of the cratering economy; I knew in 2008 that revenue at Corster, Lemp, Shreiberg, and Levine was down about 15 percent year-to-date, but I had no idea of the scope of the situation. Unfortunately, all this time later, it's hard for me to see mentions of the Great Recession without having at least a fleeting memory of Ed Horsford.

"Ashley seems pretty determined."

He shrugged. "She talks a good game." Ed was watching our spouses as he added, "Say what you will about Ash—at least she knows who wears the pants in our marriage."

I let several seconds pass, to make sure I wanted to say what I was about to say. Then I spoke as calmly as he had. "Say what you will about Jason, but at least he'd never unironically use the expression 'who wears the pants in our marriage.'"

As I left, I didn't try to catch Ashley's or Jason's attention on my way out.

The three-quarters-of-a-mile walk to the resort seemed, of course, long and dark, despite the bright stars overhead. From a block out of town on, I didn't see another person, and I wondered again about the animals that had to be all around, invisible. When the lights of the resort finally came into view, I began to run even though I was wearing a flimsy pair of flats, and I ran all the way around the main building and down the path to our cabin. I was panting as I let myself in.

After I'd brushed my teeth, I debated whether to leave the outside light on, whether Jason deserved this kindness, and decided he didn't. Then I ate both chocolates that had been left on our pillows. I must have nodded off almost immediately, and I saw on the bedside clock that close to two hours had passed when I heard Jason come in. I didn't say anything as he peed, brushed his teeth, came back out of the bathroom, and removed all his clothes except his boxers. He lifted the covers on the bed's far side before saying in a sarcastic voice, as if he'd known all along I was awake, "That was a fun night."

"It must have been if you're just getting back."

"Wait a sec—you think you get to ditch me with those two *and* be pissed that I didn't follow you?"

"I left to give you and Ashley privacy in case you wanted to take it to the next level."

"How thoughtful."

"I hope having Ed there didn't cramp your style." Neither of us spoke, and then I said, "You know that was horrible, right? For you to dance with her, that was like my high school nightmare come true." But even as I said it, I didn't exactly buy the claim myself—it felt symbolic more than true.

Jason, it seemed, thought the same. He said, "Then I guess it's lucky you're not still in high school."

We both were quiet again, until I said, "I'm sorry about my gravy train comment."

"I just don't know what I'm supposed to do to prove myself to you. Quit my job and try to get hired at a big firm so my salary is as high as yours?" He finally didn't sound sarcastic, but it was worse—he sounded deeply unhappy.

I said, "I'm glad you do what you do. It's honorable."

He laughed.

"It is," I said.

"I don't want us to keep having the same argument for the next fifty years."

"I don't either." I rolled across the bed and kissed him on the lips, and after a few seconds, he kissed me back. Then he said, "You taste like mint-chocolate-chip ice cream."

"I ate the chocolate on the pillow after I brushed my teeth. I ate yours, too."

After a silence, he said, "I'll forgive you this time. But don't let it happen again."

In the morning, I kept waking up and shutting my eyes, and I sensed Jason doing the same. At some point, I turned and saw that he was on his back, facing the ceiling. "Does your head hurt as much as mine?" I asked.

"This is what I think we should do," he said. "It's almost noon, so we'll miss the brunch here, but isn't there an IHOP or Waffle House on the outskirts of town? Let's drive there, get some grease and starch in us, then we come back here, play cribbage by the pool, and chill out. No cable car or white-water rafting or any of that stuff today."

"Deal," I said.

"One other stipulation: we don't talk any more about those fuckwads."

Beneath the sheets, I extended my hand, and we shook. "I accept the terms of your offer," I said.

Jason took a shower, then I took one, and while I dressed, he went to get the car; he said he'd meet me in front of the hotel. I walked up the path to the main building and cut through the lobby, and as soon as I stepped back outside, I saw them—they were fifteen feet away, loading suitcases into the trunk of their SUV, or Ed was loading them while Ashley talked on her phone.

I took a step backward, reflexively, just as Ashley caught sight of me and waved. We both had on sunglasses, as did Ed. Ashley held up her index finger, signaling, presumably, that I should stand there and wait for her to speak to me. I scanned the cars behind them and didn't see Jason.

"Maggie!" Ashley called, and she was pulling the phone from her ear. She wore a black cotton dress, and as she walked toward me, I thought how I'd never wear a dress on a plane—I just don't have that internal feminine calculus that makes the cuteness of a dress and bare legs seem worth the discomfort of unpredictable plane temperatures. "I'm bummed we have to leave today," she said.

I wondered if it was realistic to imagine that I could live the rest of my life without seeing her again. I'd gone sixteen years this time, which was a respectable start.

"That was so fun last night," she was saying. "And oh my God, Maggie, the dance moves on your husband! He's so adorable that if we were staying here any longer, I'd seriously have to steal him from you!"

From behind my sunglasses, I looked at her pretty thirty-three-year-old face, with its lines at the eyes and mouth. While holding my head level, maintaining her own sunglassed gaze, I bent my right leg at the knee and raised my heel behind me—I was wearing yoga pants and running shoes—and I pulled my shoelace loose. Then I swung my leg forward. "This is so weird to ask," I said, "but I think I strained a muscle in my back when we were hiking, and it hurts when I bend. Would you mind tying my shoe?"

She didn't hesitate. She said, "Oh, sure," and she leaned at the waist as I brought my right foot up and set it against her thigh. The bottom of my shoe hung off her knee, most of the sole was against her skin, and the toe overlapped with the hem of her dress. If she thought this was rude or unclean on my part, she didn't say so. As she looped the laces, she said, "What I always take for sore muscles is Advil. I don't know about you, but after last night, I could use some Advil anyway."

I didn't notice that Jason had pulled up until I heard a honk and turned my head. He, too, was wearing sunglasses, and he was watching us impassively. Although I might, over breakfast, have confessed to Jason what I'd done, to be caught in the act felt shameful.

"We gotta go, Ash," Ed called then, and I said to Ashley, "Us, too." I set my foot down, and I was the one who moved in to hug her; I did it to compensate for having ceded the high ground.

Off the Record

On the plane from Indianapolis to Los Angeles, Zoe cries so hard that a flight attendant offers to take her from Nina and carry her up and down the aisle. As Nina knew it would, the handoff, which lasts fewer than five minutes, makes Zoe cry even harder, but Nina allows it to happen as an act of contrition toward the other passengers. When they land at LAX, Zoe falls asleep inside the baby carrier that's strapped around Nina's waist and shoulders and sleeps as Nina walks off the plane, uses the bathroom, and heads to baggage claim to collect the suitcase and car seat. While Nina is trying to locate the line for taxis, Zoe wakes up enraged, so Nina finds another bathroom, sits on the toilet seat (there's no lid, and unsure if it's grosser to do this with her pants up or down, she chooses down, atop a layer of toilet paper), and nurses Zoe while the motion-detecting flusher goes off several times. When they are finally settled in a taxi, it's late afternoon in L.A.—presumably, traffic-wise, the worst time—and a pleasant sixty-five-degree October day. Zoe cries all the way to the hotel. She is six months old.

They go to sleep early and Zoe wakes only once during the night to eat, then wakes for the day at three forty-five A.M., which, to be fair, is six forty-five A.M. in Indianapolis. The sitter is not due at the hotel for another five hours. Nina eats food from home, two granola bars and a banana that has become very bruised and mushy, which Zoe declines to share. For an indeterminate but extremely long stretch, they play a game where they lie on the bed with their faces close together and Nina taps her own nose and makes a delighted gasp, then taps Zoe's nose and Zoe makes the same noise. Even after they have been up for quite some time, it's still dark outside the window of the hotel; they're in North Hollywood, and down the hill, lights are visible on the Ventura Freeway.

Nina counts, and from the time they left her mother's house (her house now, though she still isn't used to thinking of it this way) to the time they will arrive back home adds up to forty-two hours. This means that the $5,000 she is being paid to write the profile of Kelsey Adams divides into $119 an hour of travel, at least before taxes. It's not an eye-popping amount—a successful writer would be paid significantly more—but she needs the money. Although she has little confidence that she'll be able to successfully pull off the trip's logistics, it's enough to make it worth trying. Also, and somehow this feels more embarrassing than being broke, interviewing Kelsey again makes her feel like less of a loser.

Nina brought two board books to L.A., *Bear on a Bike* and *Barnyard Dance!*, and, as she always does, Zoe gazes for a particularly long time at the pages of *Bear on a Bike* on which the bear is visiting the beach. What, Nina wonders, does she see?

The first time Nina interviewed Kelsey was almost three years ago; they met for lunch in midtown Manhattan, not far from *Gloss & Glitter*'s office. The slot Nina was interviewing Kelsey for was called 3QW—Three Questions With—and would constitute a sixth of a magazine page, though Kelsey's publicist seemed to be willfully pretending that the piece would be longer and kept offering Nina increasingly elaborate "access." (They could attend a fudge-making workshop together!) Although the publicist's freneticness made Nina anticipate disliking Kelsey, Kelsey turned out to be warm, down-to-earth, and curious about Nina herself, which was rare in interview subjects. Kelsey was tickled to learn not only that Nina, too, had grown up in the Midwest but also that they shared a birthday. The day of the interview, Kelsey was twenty-eight, and Nina was thirty-one. For the previous two years, Kelsey had had a minor role on a very popular network sitcom that Nina had watched only in preparation for the interview; Kelsey played the sitcom family's mail carrier. By the time Nina's article about her ran, Kelsey had been cast as the lead in the HBO drama *Copacetic,* now in its second acclaimed season. The new movie she's starring in, which is expected to garner her an Oscar nomination, will be released at Christmas.

All of which is why, since Nina returned to Indianapolis, whenever people ask if she met anyone famous when she worked in New York, she mentions Kelsey, even though Kelsey wasn't that famous when Nina interviewed her. Nina makes a point of saying how nice Kelsey was and sometimes includes the fact that, as they were leaving the midtown restaurant, Kelsey suggested that the two of them hang out again. Nina does not include that Kelsey then added, "Is that weird?" and that Nina replied, "No, not at all," even though she *did* think it was weird—not intensely weird, but weird enough to imply that Kelsey was lonely. Mostly, Kelsey seemed to Nina young, sweet, very pretty, and neither idiotic nor particularly smart. Plus, whatever Kelsey's impression was of Nina, it wasn't accurate, because a situation in which one person is continuously asking the other questions and treating all the responses as interesting isn't representative of what it would be like for the two people to socialize. They never did hang out. The more time that has passed, the more Nina has seen her own snobby earnestness (her earnest snobbiness?) as laughably and characteristically self-sabotaging—she could have been friends with a celebrity!

Still, Nina was shocked when Astrid, her former boss from *Gloss & Glitter,* called to offer Nina the cover profile of Kelsey. First, Nina was shocked that Astrid called her in Indianapolis, something Astrid hadn't done since laying Nina off, more than a year before. Also, Nina was shocked that Astrid was offering her a major article instead of another crappy sidebar about sunscreen or PMS. And then Nina was shocked when she learned that Kelsey Adams had requested her—her, Nina, by name—to write the profile because Kelsey felt that back in 2011, they'd really "clicked."

"Your mission, should you choose to accept it, is to get her to dish on the breakup," Astrid said. Kelsey had been dating her absurdly handsome HBO costar, a dark-haired carpenter-turned-heartthrob named Scott Zaretsky, until she suddenly wasn't. And of course Nina was going to accept the assignment—she wanted the five grand.

Before they hung up, Astrid said, "How's *le bébé*?" and Nina assumed Astrid didn't remember Zoe's name. Nina had never told Astrid that she was pregnant, but someone else at the magazine had, and Astrid had sent Nina an email that said *Is this like a NYC single independent woman taking control of her fertility or an Indiana white trash baby mama fuckup :)*

Good question, Nina had emailed back.

Maybe the reason Nina wasn't offended is that she herself had wondered—still wonders—the same thing. Truly, more than she feels upset by the last few years of her life, she feels bewildered: her mother's lung cancer diagnosis; her mother's death, which was five months after she was diagnosed, four and a half months after Nina returned to Indianapolis to take care of her, and four months after (unrelatedly, Astrid assured her) Nina was laid off. By that point, Nina sort of did and sort of didn't know she was pregnant. Or she suspected, but how could she have attended to the situation while her mother was dying, even if—awkwardly, hideously—the dying took longer than Nina or even the hospice workers had expected? (She had adored her mother; every year on Nina's birthday, until she turned fifteen, Nina's mother made a mud pie out of Oreos, whipped cream, and gummy worms and served it in a real flower pot, and then she let Nina sleep that night in her queen-sized bed.) At the appointment Nina had finally made following her mother's death, when the technician estimated the pregnancy at eighteen weeks, Nina had to ask herself—as, essentially, Astrid did—if she'd waited that long on purpose. She definitely hadn't been trying to get pregnant; if she had, it wouldn't have been by a forty-seven-year-old Indianapolis lawyer she'd met at Starbucks and gone out with a total of five times, a not particularly good-looking man who had never been married and didn't want kids. (At Starbucks, Jeff had seen her doing the *Times* crossword and been condescendingly impressed.)

Their conversation about the pregnancy seemed like it belonged in an after-school special, except that the guy was thirty years too old. Their agreement is that he is giving her $1,260 a month in child support and that she has full custody of Zoe, though once every three weeks, on a Sunday, he comes over for an hour. Conveniently, it seems that none of the three of them wish for Zoe and Jeff to be alone with each other.

During that phone conversation with Astrid, Nina had been holding Zoe sideways in her right arm, Zoe's head tucked in the crook of her elbow, Nina's left pinkie in Zoe's mouth, and whenever Astrid spoke, Nina was frantically making funny faces at Zoe because, pinkie notwithstanding, Zoe was clearly on the brink of bursting into tears.

"*Le bébé* is great," Nina had said.

"Excellent," Astrid said. "Now go to California and make me proud."

Nina had planned to nurse Zoe just before leaving the hotel for the interview, after the sitter's arrival, but Zoe won't cooperate; she keeps unlatching from Nina's nipple, making eye contact with Nina, and basically smirking. "Come on, Zoe," Nina says, but Zoe continues to refuse and Nina has to leave. Riding in the taxi to Kelsey's house, she feels the way she used to before dates: Her heart is jumpy, and she keeps checking her face in the mirror of her compact, even though she knows how she looks, which is like hell.

The interview is supposed to start at ten A.M., and the taxi driver drops her off at nine forty-seven. After confirming the address, Nina is surprised by both the house's modesty and its accessibility. It's a bungalow with a steep staircase leading from the street up to the front porch, a sloping lawn planted with something that looks like a cross between grass and cacti, and no hedges or fence. Given that this is L.A.—specifically, Silver Lake—the house is no doubt worth far more than its appearance suggests. (Nina then checks on her phone and finds that Sunshine Girl LLC bought the house for $920,000 in April 2012, so presumably after Kelsey had landed the role on *Copacetic* but before its first season aired—when she probably could feel her impending fame, which is why the purchase isn't in her name, but before she was officially rich, which is why the house isn't bigger.) The funny part is that, not counting the staircase, Kelsey's house actually resembles Nina's mother's house in Indianapolis (estimated online value: $164,000).

Nina walks around the block once, then turns and walks around the block again in reverse, not passing Kelsey's house either time. All of a sudden, it's two minutes after ten. She hurries up the bungalow's staircase. As she waits, she notices security cameras in two corners of the porch, positioned near the ceiling and pointed toward where she stands. She hears a dog barking—a big dog, from the sound of it—then the unfastening of locks on the other side of the door, and then Kelsey Adams is standing in front of her, impossibly beautiful, wearing a gardenia-scented perfume Nina can smell through the screen.

"Hi!" Kelsey says. She hugs Nina, and Nina wishes she had access to the footage in the security cameras and could post this hug on Facebook. Not really, of course— Nina tries to look at Facebook as infrequently as possible—but it's strangely vindicating: Something Nina has for almost three years pretended to herself and others, which is that she and Kelsey Adams could have been friends, almost were friends, might be true.

The dog, a massive white Great Pyrenees, keeps appearing on either side of Kelsey's legs, barking and sniffing, and Kelsey laughs and says, "Calm down, Chester." To Nina, she says, "Sorry, he gets excited by visitors."

"He's fine," Nina says and steps inside as Kelsey says to Chester in a tone of singsongy affection, "Can you just chill out for one minute? Can you?"

Chester barks, and Kelsey says, "I'll put him in the kitchen."

From the alcove inside the front door, Nina sees an impeccably decorated living room—two white couches, a glass coffee table with a vase of white tulips in its center— and beyond that a dining room and a swinging door, through which Kelsey and Chester disappear. The house is bigger than it looks from the outside, and Nina has the sense that no one is in it besides Kelsey, no housekeeper or assistant.

In Kelsey's absence, Nina ponders whether she should

enter the living room and sit down or continue standing near the front door. She opts for the latter, and when Kelsey returns, she says, "Oh my God, come on in! Make yourself at home." Kelsey is holding two glasses of ice water, which she sets on the coffee table. She sits on a couch and tucks her legs sideways on the cushions. It doesn't serve a purpose to think this, but since they last saw each other, Nina suspects that she has gained the exact amount of weight that Kelsey has lost, which is seventeen pounds. When Nina was pregnant, she actually gained more like thirty pounds, so she's no longer as big as she was, but she's still at the high end of her nonpregnant weight. All that stuff about how breast-feeding speeds up your metabolism is, she's pretty sure, bullshit.

As for Kelsey, she's now as thin as she could be without her thinness seeming alarming, or maybe it *is* alarming. Maybe in real life it's alarming, but she still looks good on-screen. Her hair is white-blond, her eyes big and blue, her skin creamy—as creamy as a baby's, or so Nina might have thought before giving birth to Zoe, whose eczema often causes her to scratch her own forehead while wailing, especially at bedtime.

As Nina sets her bag on the white carpet and sits on the other couch, Kelsey says, "This is so fun, right? How have you been?"

It seems safe to assume that, just as Nina and Kelsey have gained and lost inverse amounts of weight, Nina knows the exact amount about Kelsey that Kelsey doesn't know about her—that Kelsey believes, insofar as she's given it any thought, that Nina still lives in New York and works full-time at *Gloss & Glitter*. This interview was arranged via approximately forty emails among Nina, *Gloss*

& Glitter's executive editor, *Gloss & Glitter*'s on-staff celebrity wrangler, Kelsey's publicist, and the publicist's assistant, whom Nina imagines was also communicating with Kelsey's assistant. The outcome of all the emails was that on Thursday, October 23, 2014, for the cover story of *Gloss & Glitter*'s February issue, Nina would interview—is interviewing—Kelsey from ten to eleven A.M. at her home, followed by a forty-five-minute walk around the Silver Lake Reservoir, after which Nina and Kelsey will immediately part ways because Kelsey has an important call at noon. (No fudge-making workshops for anyone this time.)

"Oh, please," Nina says in what she hopes is a breezy tone. "Who cares about me? Congratulations on all the amazing stuff that's happened to *you*." As Nina pulls her digital recorder from the blue leather satchel she hasn't used since she lived in New York and sets the recorder on the coffee table, she adds, "Your house is gorgeous."

"I'm moving next week," Kelsey says. "I'll miss this place, though."

"Where are you moving?"

When their eyes meet, Nina sees Kelsey's wariness. "Up into the hills," Kelsey says and gestures vaguely. "West." Nina wonders if Kelsey has stalkers.

"Have you been back to Michigan lately?" Nina asks.

"I went for the Fourth of July, which was really nice and relaxing. But my schedule has been so insane lately that it's easier for my family to come here. My new house has a mother-in-law suite, and I've told my family they're welcome anytime. My parents are terrified of driving on the freeway, but even that, I'm like, You can Uber every-where." Kelsey smiles, and really, she's so outrageously pretty that it would have been a waste for her *not* to appear on-screen. This is what Nina is thinking when, in her pocket, her phone vibrates. She's sure it's the sitter—in normal life, no one texts her anymore—and she's also sure that she shouldn't interrupt the interview just when it's starting. Besides, isn't Kelsey too famous for Nina to check her phone in front of her? Kelsey fondly adds, "As if Bill and Barbara Adams of Traverse City, Michigan, even grasp what Uber is."

Nina fake-laughs, and her phone vibrates a second time. "So all the Oscar buzz has to feel good," she says, and again Kelsey's smile is guarded.

"Obviously, it's really unpredictable how things will play out," Kelsey says. "I mean, the film is still six weeks away from release. But it's thrilling that people are responding to it so positively. And working with Ira Barbour was a dream come true. Walking onto the set every day, I had to pinch myself."

"Are there any moments from the shoot that really stand out for you?"

Kelsey pauses before saying, "I'm guessing you know Scott and I broke up recently?"

What a surprise, what a tremendous relief, that Kelsey has broached the topic on her own. It's actually a double surprise, because Scott is her TV costar; he has nothing to do with the movie. Nina strives not to sound pleased as she says, "Yeah, I did hear about that. How are you doing?"

Without warning, Kelsey bursts into tears—her beautiful face crumples in on itself, and rivulets cascade from her blue eyes.

"Oh no," Nina says. "Oh, I'm so sorry."

Kelsey sobs, says, "I'm just—" and then waves her left hand instead of speaking. She stands and walks to a shelf, where she pulls a tissue from a box between artfully arranged books. She blows her nose and, as she walks back to the couch, says, surprisingly coherently, "I swore to myself I wouldn't cry. But when I talk to you, I feel like I'm hanging out with one of my girlfriends from high school."

"Well, being upset about a breakup is natural," Nina says. "You *are* human."

"I'll tell you the truth," Kelsey says. "Scott and I were secretly engaged. Also, I was pregnant."

Oh, Astrid, Nina thinks. *You're welcome.*

"It wasn't on purpose," Kelsey is saying, "but we were both really excited. And so he proposes, and Scott isn't a super-emotional person, but the proposal was incredibly sweet. He said he was so happy he'd found someone else who was grounded and had good values and he wanted us to be a team and support each other in the crazy world of L.A. Five weeks later, I miscarried, and literally the next day he moved out. I'm not even exaggerating. Then those paparazzi pictures show up of him with Amanda St. Clair, and you can tell they were staged because they're totally dressed up, practically smiling at the camera while they make out, and it's like, What the hell? Fine if he didn't really want to be with me, but I have no idea why he had to rub it in my face." Kelsey makes an enormous sniffing noise. "At some point, he's being such a sociopath that I really am better off without him. But when he proposed, it felt real." Kelsey has been gazing into the middle distance, but she turns her head to the left, making eye contact again with Nina and says, "The baby was due in early March, and that's why whenever someone brings up the Oscars, all I can think about is stuff with Scott. I would have been majorly pregnant for awards season." She frowns a little before adding, "Is it weird I'm telling you all this?"

That Kelsey will retroactively declare everything she just said off the record is a possibility so terrifying that Nina almost can't breathe. Not that it will be exactly, explicitly binding even if Kelsey does, but it would be kind of shitty of Nina to take advantage of Kelsey's naïveté, plus *Gloss & Glitter* will want to maintain its friendly relationship with Kelsey's publicist and agent and the rest of her professional constellation. Of course, *Gloss & Glitter*—Astrid—also will be disgustingly thrilled to break the news of Kelsey's miscarriage, which is why Nina must proceed very, very carefully.

In a light but sympathetic voice, she says, "It's not weird at all. What you went through—that sounds so hard."

Kelsey says, "Not to be, like, too personal, but have you ever had a miscarriage?"

Nina shakes her head.

"They're brutal," Kelsey says. "I used to think of them as not such a big deal, but they're completely awful. My ob told me I could have a D&C in his office or I could wait at home and pass the fetus naturally, and he made it sound like six of one, a half dozen of the other, but I definitely should have had the procedure."

"I'm sorry," Nina says again. "I'm really sorry."

"It's like going through labor. You have real contractions that are super-painful, and you even have to push, but all that comes out is tons and tons of blood. And, you know, the gestational sac. My bathroom looked like

a murder scene. Scott is really squeamish, and I swear that
if he hadn't seen all that blood, we'd still be together."

For several reasons, Nina thinks, Kelsey needs to
stop—for one, because the more detail she goes into, the
more likely it is she'll want to retract everything. Also, the
readers of *Gloss & Glitter* will be enthralled/concerned
to learn of Kelsey's miscarriage but concerned/grossed
out to hear about its effluvia. And finally, listening to
Kelsey is making Nina feel an urgent need to check the
sitter's texts and confirm that Zoe is okay.

"That does sound awful." Nina furrows her brow—
kindly, she hopes. "I can't even imagine. Are you and
Scott in touch at all?"

Kelsey shakes her head.

"But filming for season three of *Copacetic* starts next
week, right?"

Kelsey shrugs. "I know. And what can I do but cross
that bridge when I come to it, right?"

"Sorry to—" Nina hesitates, then says, "Is it okay if I
use your bathroom?"

Kelsey's guest bathroom looks nothing like the guest
bathroom in Nina's mother's house—Kelsey's is very
clean, with lots of white marble surfaces (surely, the bathroom where she bled so voluminously is nearer to her
bedroom). Nina sets down the lid of the toilet, sits, and
pulls her phone from her pocket.

She has been crying since you left, reads the first text.

Followed almost immediately by: *She will not take any
food*

Nina's heart, which had slowed on entering Kelsey's
house, begins hammering again. She texts back, *Did you
try jar of pears?*

The response is instantaneous: *I have tried everything*

Nina types, *Maybe go outside with her? She likes looking at birds.*

The fact that so many things displease Zoe—Nina doesn't entirely fault her for it. Many things displease Nina, too, and she has far more control over her life than Zoe has over hers.

Keep me posted, Nina texts, then stands and, in case Kelsey is listening, flushes. She feels the first ache of fullness in her breasts, an ache that very possibly is psychosomatic and babysitter-text induced. She should have worn breast pads in case she starts leaking, she thinks, but she forgot to even bring any to California.

Back in the living room, Kelsey smiles sheepishly and says, "Now that I've totally derailed things, do you want to go get breakfast? Are you hungry?"

Nina hasn't eaten since the granola bars and banana almost seven hours ago in her hotel room; she's ravenous. She says, "Breakfast sounds perfect."

They go to a place that's a diner except that their omelets are, respectively, twenty-two and twenty-seven dollars. The restaurant is a couple miles from Kelsey's house, and Kelsey drove them both there in, as Nina dutifully jotted down in her notebook, a black Porsche Cayenne hybrid. As Nina also dutifully jots down, Kelsey's omelet is egg whites only, with spinach and mushrooms, and she eats a third of it and doesn't touch her toast or potatoes; not that the world will care, but Nina's omelet is yolks-in, with tomatoes, sausage, and cheese, and she eats all of it, plus the toast and potatoes. They discuss Kelsey's TV show and her movie, which was shot in Kentucky and South Africa, and another movie she's about to star in, and actors and directors Kelsey would like to work with. Even though Nina knows that after she returns to Indianapolis, Kelsey will again seem glamorous, the truth is that, as they sit inches apart, Nina agrees with her own impression from three years ago: Kelsey isn't particularly bright or interesting. Neither of them brings up the topic of Scott. Nina can feel some of the restaurant's staff and other patrons registering an awareness of Kelsey's presence, can feel Kelsey feeling it, and she plans to ask what this phenomenon is like.

It is while Kelsey is explaining why a particular romantic comedy is her favorite movie that Nina's phone vibrates in her pocket, three times in a row.

"Literally, I've watched it a hundred times," Kelsey says. "The part at the end where he tells her he's dreamed of her every night since they last saw each other? *So swoony.*"

"Sorry, but I need to use the restroom again." As Nina stands, she gestures at her empty plate and Kelsey's mostly full one and, in an excessively cheerful voice that reminds her of her mother's, then makes her sad because her mother has now been dead for a year, Nina says, "Delicious!"

She has not stopped crying, the first text from the babysitter reads.

I tried taking her outside it did not work
She does not have fever but do u think she's sick

There is a part of Nina—say, 15 percent of her—that thinks, *For Christ's sake, what am I paying you for?* The sitter works for an agency that charged Nina a two-hundred-dollar fee to join, before the twenty-eight dollars an hour she is paying the sitter herself. This is roughly four times the going rate in Indianapolis, not that Nina has ever used a sitter back home. And, of course, *Gloss & Glitter* isn't covering the expense—the magazine wouldn't have regardless, but Nina didn't tell Astrid she was taking Zoe to Los Angeles.

Meanwhile, the other 85 percent of Nina cannot bear listening to Kelsey Adams prattle as her daughter cries in the care of a seemingly incompetent stranger. It's not that she symbolically can't bear it, it's actually physical—she feels like jumping out of her skin. Plus, Nina's breasts are now so swollen that she's tempted to manually pump them, but where? And into what?

On the phone's screen, Nina sees that it's eleven-fifty, which means the interview is about to end, apparently without the walk around the reservoir. Nina considers trying to FaceTime the sitter and Zoe from the bathroom, but, like manually pumping, this idea seems like it could create more problems than it solves.

Nina rejoins Kelsey at the table but doesn't sit. "I know you have a call at noon," she says. "It's great hearing about everything you've been up to."

Kelsey looks confused. "Aren't we going for a walk?"

"Oh, I assumed since we had breakfast . . ." Nina trails off, then smiles to compensate. Of course Kelsey doesn't really have a call.

"Do you have something else planned?" Kelsey still sounds confused but also a little pointed now.

"No!" Nina says and sits. "Are you finished eating? I just wasn't sure if you were finished." In her pocket, her phone buzzes yet again.

"I want more coffee," Kelsey says and raises a hand in the direction of the waitress, who comes over quickly.

Nina had paused her recorder before going to the bathroom. She starts it again and says, "So where do you see yourself in five years?"

"Professionally or personally?" Kelsey asks.

"Either," Nina says. "Both." While Kelsey is speaking, Nina pulls her phone from her pocket—it's 2014, people do this, fuck Kelsey's fame—and the text reads, *In my 22 years as a care provider this is the most a baby has ever cried*

"I know it's such a cliché, but I'd love to try directing," Kelsey is saying. "One of my role models—"

"You know what?" Nina interrupts. "I do have to go. I really apologize, but I—I—" She pauses, and Kelsey looks at her. "I have a baby, and I need to go nurse her."

Kelsey seems bewildered. "You have a baby?"

"In my hotel room," Nina says. "She's six months old. I never got her to take a bottle—I messed up, I have no idea what I was thinking. But she won't take one, and she's really finicky about jar food, and she needs to eat now."

This is when, as if to offer proof—as if proof is necessary, as if anyone would lie about such a failure—Nina's milk lets down. There's that hardening in her nipples, then the release, the liquid spilling in two warm, fast lines, immediately soaking through her bra and shirt. Kelsey looks as if she has detected a bad smell. But when Kelsey speaks, her voice is dispassionate, almost clinically curious. She says, "Why didn't you tell me before?"

Nina tries to sound respectful, not defensive, when she says, "You didn't ask if I'd had a baby."

Because it would have been self-centered and insensitive

to tell you, Nina thinks. *And because I didn't realize Zoe's existence would become relevant. And because you don't care.* Aloud, she says, "My daughter isn't really used to people besides me. I'm sorry that I didn't plan this better, but I'll order a taxi back to my hotel."

"Just Uber."

"I don't have Uber on my phone."

"Where are you staying?"

"North Hollywood."

"I'll drive you," Kelsey says. "If you're trying to get there as fast as possible." Even if there isn't apparent sympathy in her tone, Kelsey is offering a favor, and Nina is not in a position to decline it. As she sets cash on the table and they walk out of the restaurant, she knows that without the check, she won't be reimbursed by *Gloss & Glitter.*

I'm coming back to hotel now, Nina texts the babysitter from the passenger seat of Kelsey's SUV. *About 15 min.*

Then Nina turns on her recorder and says, "So your dream kiss, on-screen or off—who would it be?"

Kelsey turns to look at her with an expression that is unmistakably appalled. Which Nina understands, but at the same time, it's *Gloss & Glitter*'s signature question; the magazine's writers ask this of all the subjects of cover profiles, even the occasional athlete. And getting a follow-up answer from a famous subject, after the interview, is a hundred times harder than getting it in the moment.

Coldly, Kelsey says, "Hmm. I'd have to think about that." For several minutes, they listen to a pop channel on satellite radio, not speaking.

Kelsey has just turned off Santa Monica Boulevard when she says, "That stuff I told you about Scott and our breakup and the miscarriage—obviously, I didn't mean for it to be in the article." She sounds calm and certain, not nervous.

Fuck, Nina thinks. She says, "Oh, I promise I'll handle it in a very respectful way."

"After I specially requested you to write this piece, it would be a bummer to find out that I shouldn't have trusted you," Kelsey says, and there is in her tone a new steeliness, possibly a menacing quality—*a bummer for you* is the implication. Even so, if there were not two still-widening lines of breast milk running down the front of Nina's shirt, if Kelsey were not chauffeuring her, surely she would say delicate and suasive things. At least she'd try.

As it is, Nina says, "I hear you."

The hotel where Nina is staying has a circular driveway in front, with a fountain in the center. When Kelsey pulls into the driveway, Nina sees that the sitter and Zoe are standing outside. The sitter has Zoe propped on her right hip, and Zoe is big-cheeked and little-nosed, mostly bald, her plump arms emerging from a sleeveless pink shirt with a fish on it, her squat little legs bent in yellow pants, her feet bare.

Nina is surprised that they're outside and more surprised that Zoe is not crying. To be sure, her expression is one of annoyance. But it's also one of scrutiny and discernment. Even spending all day in a house with her, Nina is often caught off guard by the intelligence in her daughter's eyes, and as they approach the hotel, from thirty feet away—that is, before it's really possible—Nina feels that this intelligence is trained on her.

While still sitting next to Kelsey in the front seat, Nina understands that she will never see Kelsey again. They aren't friends, they never were friends, they never will be. Nina will never again interview a celebrity. In fact, she will never again write for *Gloss & Glitter* or any other magazine. This part she doesn't know, but six weeks from now—which, not coincidentally, will be ten days before her COBRA insurance expires—she will accept a grant-writing job at a nonprofit; she will enroll Zoe in daycare; Zoe will cry nonstop for the first six days and then, abruptly, be fine.

Kelsey will indeed be nominated for an Oscar; she won't win, but four months from now, at the ceremony, she will present the award for Best Documentary Feature, and people who pay attention to such things will agree that her dress, a sheer ice-blue gown by Dior Haute Couture, is one of the night's best. In the weeks prior to and following the Oscars, she will be everywhere in the media, her wardrobe and hairstyles, her upcoming projects, her girlish midwestern charm. And in a taped interview that airs just before the Oscars and is conducted by a legendary octogenarian television personality, an interview Nina will watch lying in bed while Zoe sits next to her eating oyster crackers from a purple plastic cup, Kelsey will tearfully describe the miscarriage she suffered in September 2014.

"I hadn't gotten pregnant on purpose, but we were both really excited," Kelsey will say. "And Scott isn't a super-emotional person, but his proposal was incredibly sweet. He said how he was so happy he'd found someone else who was grounded and had good values and he wanted us to be a team and support each other in the crazy world of L.A. Then five weeks later I miscarried, and literally the next day he moved out. And then those paparazzi pictures show up of him with—" This time, Kelsey will roll her eyes but not say Amanda St. Clair's name. Also, she won't describe all the blood, and Nina will wonder if one of her handlers advised against it, or if these are edits Kelsey made on her own. For the part when Kelsey said to Nina that she swore she wouldn't cry but she felt like she was hanging out with one of her girlfriends from high school, Kelsey will amend it to "But I feel like I'm hanging out with my favorite auntie in Michigan." Which is tactful, given that the interviewer is probably the age of Kelsey's grandmother.

How astonished Nina will be to realize not only that Kelsey has fucked her over but that in complying with Kelsey's request, Nina herself was showing stupidity rather than compassion. How astonishing Kelsey's shrewdness will be—it will elicit from Nina genuine respect, along with a predictable antipathy. Given that Nina's career as a journalist is finished, however, does it really make a difference? Defying Kelsey could have prolonged Nina's career, but probably not by much.

As Kelsey turns her SUV into the hotel driveway, she says, still coldly, "Did you think I'd be jealous?" Nina is about to say no, which is the truth, when Kelsey adds, "Of you?"

But cranky, suspicious, eczema-ridden Zoe—Nina loves her so much! She's so happy to see her! Outside the hotel, perched on the sitter's hip, wearing her undignified clothes, Zoe is very familiar and dear, and it occurs to Nina that today is the first time she's ever had the chance to miss her daughter.

The Prairie Wife

The understanding is that, after Casey's iPhone alarm goes off at 6:15 A.M., Kirsten wakes the boys, nudges them to get dressed, and herds them downstairs, all while Casey is showering. The four of them eat breakfast as a family, deal with teeth brushing and backpacks, and Casey, who is the principal of the middle school in the same district as the elementary school Jack and Ian attend, drives the boys to drop-off. Kirsten then takes her shower in the newly quiet house before leaving for work.

The reality is that, at 6:17, as soon as Casey shuts the bathroom door, Kirsten grabs her own iPhone from her nightstand and looks at Lucy Headrick's Twitter feed. Clearly, Kirsten is not alone: Lucy has 3.1 million followers. (She follows a mere 533 accounts, many of which belong to fellow celebrities.) Almost all of Lucy's vast social-media empire, which, of course, is an extension of her lifestyle-brand empire (whatever the fuck a lifestyle brand is), drives Kirsten crazy. Its content is fake and pandering and boring and repetitive—how many times will Lucy post variations on the same recipe for buttermilk biscuits?—and Kirsten devours all of it, every day: Facebook and Instagram, Tumblr and Pinterest, the blog, the vlog, the TV show. Every night, Kirsten swears that she won't devote another minute to Lucy, and every day she squanders hours.

The reason things go wrong so early in the morning, she has realized, is this: She's pretty sure Twitter is the only place where real, actual Lucy is posting, Lucy whom Kirsten once knew. Lucy has insomnia, and while all the other posts on all the other sites might be written by Lucy's minions, Kirsten is certain that it was Lucy herself who, at 1:22 A.M., wrote, "Watching Splash on cable, oops I forgot to name one of my daughters Madison!" Or, at 3:14 A.M., accompanied by a photo of an organic candy bar: "Hmm could habit of eating chocolate in middle of night be part of reason I can't sleep LOL!"

Morning, therefore, is when there's new, genuine Lucy sustenance. So how can Kirsten resist? And then the day is Lucy-contaminated already, and there's little incentive for Kirsten not to keep polluting it for the sixteen hours until she goes to bed with the bullshitty folksiness in Lucy's life: the acquisition of an Alpine goat, the canning of green beans, the baby shower that Lucy is planning for her young friend Jocelyn, who lives on a neighboring farm.

As it happens, Lucy has written (or "written," right? There's no way) a memoir, with recipes—*Dishin' with the Prairie Wife*—that is being published today, so Kirsten's latest vow is that she'll buy the book (she tried to reserve it from the library and learned that she was 305th in line), read it, and then be done with Lucy. Completely. Forever.

The memoir has been "embargoed"—as if Lucy is, like, Henry Kissinger—and, to promote it, Lucy traveled yesterday from her farm in Missouri to Los Angeles. (As she told Twitter, "BUMMM-PEE flyin over the mountains!!") Today she will appear on a hugely popular TV talk show on which she has been a guest more than once. Among last night's tweets, posted while Kirsten was sleeping, was the following: "Omigosh you guys I'm so nervous + excited for Mariana!!! Wonder what she will ask . . ." The pseudo-nervousness, along with the "Omigosh"—never "Omigod" or even "OMG"—galls Kirsten. Twenty years ago, Lucy swore like a normal person, but the Lucy of now, Kirsten thinks, resembles Casey, who, when their sons were younger, respectfully asked Kirsten to stop cursing in front of them. Indeed, the Lucy of now—beloved by evangelicals, homeschooler of her three daughters, wife of a man she refers to as the Stud in Overalls, who is a deacon in their church—uses such substitutes as "Jiminy Crickets!" and "Fudge nuggets!" Once, while making a custard on the air, Lucy dropped a bit of eggshell into the mix and exclaimed, "Shnookerdookies!" Kirsten assumed that it was staged, or maybe not originally staged but definitely not edited out when it could have been. This made Kirsten feel such rage at Lucy that it was almost like lust.

Kirsten sees that last night, Lucy, as she usually does, replied to a few dozen tweets sent to her by nobodies, including Nicole in Seattle, who has thirty-one followers, and Tara in Jacksonville, who's the mom of two awesome boys. (Aren't we all? Kirsten thinks.) Most of the fans' tweets say some variation of "You're so great!" or "It's my birthday pretty please wish me a happy birthday?!" Most of Lucy's responses say some variation of "Thank you for the kind words!" or "Happy Birthday!" Kirsten has never tweeted at Lucy; in fact, Kirsten has never tweeted. Her Twitter handle is not her name but "Minneap" plus the last three digits of her zip code, and instead of uploading a photo of herself, she's kept the generic egg avatar. She has three followers, all of whom appear to be bots.

Through the bathroom door, Kirsten can hear the shower running, and the minute Casey turns it off—by this point, Kirsten is, as she also does daily, reading an article about how smartphones are destroying people's ability to concentrate—she springs from bed, flicking on light switches in the master bedroom, the hall, and the boys' rooms. When Casey appears, wet hair combed, completely dressed, and finds Ian still under the covers and Kirsten standing by his bureau, Kirsten frowns and says that both boys seem really tired this morning. Casey nods somberly, even though it's what Kirsten says every morning. Is Casey clueless, inordinately patient, or both?

At breakfast, Jack, who is six, asks, "Do doctors ever get sick?"

"Of course," Casey says. "Everyone gets sick."

While packing the boys' lunches, Kirsten says to Ian, who is nine, "I'm giving you Oreos again today, but you need to eat your cucumber slices, and if they're still in your lunch box when you come home, you don't get Oreos tomorrow."

She kisses the three of them goodbye, and as soon as the door closes, even before she climbs the stairs, Kirsten knows that she's going to get herself off using the hand-held showerhead. She doesn't consider getting herself off using the handheld showerhead morally problematic, but it presents two logistical complications, the first of which is that, the more often she does it, the more difficult it is for Casey to bring her to orgasm on the occasions when they're feeling ambitious enough to have sex. The second complication is that it makes her late for work. If Kirsten leaves the house at 7:45, she has a fifteen-minute drive; if she leaves at or after 7:55, the drive is twice as long. But, seriously, what else is she supposed to do with her Lucy rage?

Kirsten's commute is when she really focuses on whether she has the power to destroy Lucy Headrick's life. Yes, the question hums in the background at other moments, like when Kirsten is at the grocery store and sees a cooking magazine with Lucy on the cover—it's just so fucking weird how famous Lucy is—but it's in the car that Kirsten thinks through, in a realistic way, which steps she'd take. She's figured out where she could leak the news and has narrowed it down to two gossip websites, both based in Manhattan; she's even found the "Got tips?" link on one. If she met somebody who worked for such a site, and if the person promised she could remain anonymous, it would be tempting. But, living in Minneapolis, Kirsten will never meet anyone who works for a Manhattan gossip website.

Kirsten's co-worker Frank has volunteered to leak the

news for her; indeed, he's so eager that she fears he might do it without her blessing, except that he knows she knows he pads his expense reports when he travels. And it's Frank's joyous loathing of Lucy that reins in Kirsten's own antipathy. Frank has never met the woman, so what reason does he have to hate her? Because she's successful? This, in Kirsten's opinion, isn't sufficient. Kirsten hates Lucy Headrick because she's a hypocrite.

In 1994, the summer after their freshman year in college, Kirsten and Lucy were counselors at a camp in northern Minnesota. It was coed, and Kirsten was assigned to the Redbirds cabin, girls age nine, while Lucy was with the Bluejays, age eleven. Back then, Lucy weighed probably twenty-five pounds more than she does now, had very short light brown hair, and had affixed a triangle-shaped rainbow pin to her backpack. The first night, at the counselors' orientation before the campers arrived, she said, "As a lesbian, one of my goals this summer is to make sure all the kids feel comfortable being who they are." Kirsten knew a few gay students at her Jesuit college, but not well, and Lucy was the first peer she'd heard use the word *lesbian* other than as a slur. Although Kirsten took a mild prurient interest in Lucy's disclosure, she was mostly preoccupied with the hotness of a counselor named Sean, who was very tall and could play "Welcome to the Jungle" on the guitar. Sean never reciprocated Kirsten's interest; instead, and this felt extra insulting, he soon took up with the other counselor in the Redbirds cabin.

Kirsten became conscious of Lucy's crush on her without paying much attention to it. Having given the subject a great deal of thought since, Kirsten now believes

that she was inattentive partly because of her vague discomfort and partly because she was busy wondering if
Sean and Renee would break up and, if they did, how
she, Kirsten, would make her move.

Lucy often approached Kirsten, chattily, at all-camp
events or when the counselors drank and played cards at
night in the mess hall, and, more than once, she tried to
initiate deep conversations Kirsten had no interest in.
("Do you believe in soul mates?" or "Do you usually
have more regrets about things you've done or things
you haven't done?") When Kirsten and Lucy ran into
each other on the fourth-to-last night of camp, on the
path behind the arts-and-crafts shed, when they were
both drunk, it was maybe not as random or spontaneous
as it seemed, at least on Lucy's part. Kirsten had never
kissed a girl, though she'd had sex with one boy in high
school and another in college, and she's wondered if
she'd have kissed just about anyone she ran into behind
the shed. She was nineteen, it was August, she was drunk,
and she felt like taking off her clothes. That it all seemed
especially hot with Lucy didn't strike her then as that
meaningful. They hooked up in the dark, on a ratty red
couch, in a room that smelled like the kiln and tempera
paint. Kirsten was definitely aware of the variables of
there being more than one set of boobs smashed together
and the peculiarly untroubling absence of an erection,
but there were things she heard later about two girls—
about how soft the female body was and how good another girl smelled—that seemed to her like nonsense. She
and Lucy rolled around a lot, and jammed their fingers
up inside each other, and, though both of them had
probably swum in the lake that day, neither was freshly

showered. There really wasn't much in the way of soft-
ness or fragrant scents about the encounter. What she
liked was how close they could be, almost fused, with
nothing between them.

The next morning, while Kirsten was standing by the
orange juice dispenser in the mess hall, Lucy approached
her, set a hand on her forearm, and said, softly, "Hey."

Kirsten, who was intensely hungover and sleep-
deprived, recoiled, and she saw Lucy see her recoil. "I'm
not gay," Kirsten muttered.

If Lucy had done anything other than laugh light-
heartedly, that might have halted things. But Lucy's willingness to act as if neither their hookup nor Kirsten's
homophobia were a big deal—it made it seem okay to
keep going. The whole whatever-it-was was so clearly
short-lived, so arbitrary.

During the next five nights—the counselors stayed an
extra forty-eight hours to clean the grounds after the kids
went home—Kirsten and Lucy were naked together a
lot. The second night was both the first time someone
went down on Kirsten and the first time she had an orgasm; the orgasm part happened more than once. She
was less drunk than the night before, and at one point,
while Lucy was lapping away at her, she thought that, all
things considered, it was good that it was happening with
a girl first, because then when a guy went down on her,
when it mattered, Kirsten would know what she was
doing.

After Kirsten had basically spasmed in ecstasy into Lucy's face, she said, "Could you tell I'd never done that?"

It was less that Kirsten was confiding than that, with
Lucy, she didn't feel the need to feign competence.

Lucy was lying on top of her, propped up on her elbows, and she seemed amused—flirtatious-amused, not mean-amused—as she said, "Seriously? Never?"

Kirsten said, "Well, I've given blow jobs."

"Then that *really* doesn't seem fair."

The sureness of Lucy's hooking-up personality, the way it might even have been more confident than her regular personality, impressed Kirsten; the nearest Kirsten got to such confidence was when things felt so good that she forgot herself.

Lucy added, "Just in case none of the recipients of your blow jobs ever mentioned it, you're very, very fun to have sex with," and Kirsten said, "This isn't sex."

As she had by the juice dispenser, Lucy laughed. "I mean, it's fooling around," Kirsten said. "I'm not denying that."

"You think if there's no penis, it doesn't count?"

Lucy's apparent lack of anger surprises Kirsten more in retrospect than it did at the time. Lucy explained that she was a gold-star lesbian, which meant one who'd never had sex with a guy; in fact, Lucy added proudly, she'd never even kissed a guy. Kirsten asked how she'd known she was gay, and Lucy said, "Because, even when I was in grade school, the people I always thought about before I fell asleep at night were girls."

That what was transpiring between them would be kept secret was both understood and probably not very realistic. Before they lay down on the red couch, Kirsten would block the door with a chair, but sometimes dim figures, other couples in search of privacy, opened the door partway. When this happened, Kirsten would freeze, and Lucy would call out sharply, "There are people in here," and a retreat would occur. Once, someone very tall opened the door all the way and just stood there, not moving, someone else behind him, and Kirsten realized, with one of her nipples in Lucy's mouth, that the person in front was Sean, and Kirsten's fixation with him, a fixation that had lasted until just a few days before, seemed distant. Lucy lifted her head and said, in a firm voice, "Can you please leave?" Sean and Renee did go away, but the next morning Renee asked, with what seemed more like curiosity than disapproval, "Was that you with Lucy?"

All these years later, while driving to work and considering ruining Lucy's life, Kirsten thinks that Renee would be her corroboration, and maybe Sean, too. Conveniently, Kirsten is Facebook friends with both of them, privy to the extremely tedious details of their separate suburban lives.

At the time, fake-casually, fake-confusedly, Kirsten said, "With who?"

That fall, back at school, Kirsten opened her mailbox in the student union one day to find a small padded envelope, the return address Lucy's, the contents a brief, unremarkable note ("Hope you're having a good semester . . .") and a mixtape. Kirsten was surprised and very happy, which made her inability to listen to the mixtape perplexing; the first song was "I Melt with You," and the second line of the song was "Making love to you was never second best," and though she tried several times not to, Kirsten always had to turn off her cassette player after that line. She never acknowledged Lucy's gift.

The next summer, Kirsten returned to the camp, and Lucy didn't; someone said that she was volunteering at a health clinic in Haiti. Kirsten had a boyfriend then, a guy named Ryan, who was working in the admissions office of their college and to whom she hadn't mentioned Lucy.

After that summer, Kirsten's only source of camp updates was a winter newsletter, which she read less and less thoroughly as the years passed. She became aware of the Prairie Wife, in the amorphous way one becomes aware of celebrities, without having any idea that Lucy Headrick was Lucy from camp, whose surname had been Nilsson. She even saw pictures of Lucy online and in magazines and didn't recognize her. But last December, Kirsten read the camp newsletter in its entirety. It was the day after Christmas, and she was trying to get Jack to take a nap, which he didn't do much anymore, but he'd been cranky, and they were due at a potluck in the evening. She was sitting halfway up the steps of their house so as to intercept Jack whenever he tried to escape from his room; she'd pulled the newsletter from a stack of mail by the front door to occupy herself between interceptions.

The camp had been owned by the same family for several generations, and an eccentric great-uncle who taught archery wrote the newsletter. The item about Lucy was just a paragraph and not particularly fawning—"It's always fun to see what former camper and counselor Lucy 'the Prairie Wife' Headrick née Lucy Nilsson is up to"—but Kirsten couldn't believe it. Though she didn't own any of Lucy Headrick's cookbooks and had never seen her television show, she knew enough about her to find it hilarious. She knew that Lucy Headrick was gorgeous (she had long blond hair and magnificent cheekbones), was married to a man, and was, in some conservative-flavored way, religious. Kirsten was so excited to tell Casey that she let Jack get out of bed. They went into the den, where Casey and Ian were watching football, Kirsten carrying the camp newsletter. But it turned out that although Kirsten had mentioned Lucy to Casey, Casey had never heard of the Prairie Wife, so Kirsten's ostensible bombshell was less satisfying to drop than she'd anticipated.

That might have been that—a funny coincidence—except that a week later, at the digital-map-data company where she works, Kirsten passed Frank's office while he was watching Lucy Headrick make chicken-and-dumpling soup online. "I'm decompressing," Frank said. "I just turned in a test tally."

Kirsten held up her palms and said, "Hey, no judgment." She almost didn't say it, but then, pointing at the computer screen, she did. "I kind of know her."

Frank raised one eyebrow, which was a gesture Kirsten suspected he had, in his adolescence, practiced at great length. Frank was her age, the son of Thai immigrants, and he was married to a white guy who was a dermatologist. Kirsten liked Frank okay—she respected his attention to detail—but she didn't really trust him.

Frank said, "Do go on."

She tried to think of reasons that not trusting Frank mattered and couldn't come up with any. Once, she had considered her hook-ups with Lucy to be her most damning secret, but now, ironically, they were probably the most interesting thing about her, even if Casey had been underwhelmed.

"I haven't seen her since the mid-nineties, but we worked at a camp a few hours north of here," Kirsten said, then added, "We slept together a bunch of times."

"No. Fucking. Way." Frank looked elated. He made a lascivious "Mm-mm-mm" sound and said, "You and the Prairie Wife as baby dykes. I love it."

"Actually," Kirsten said, "I looked it up, and I'm pretty sure Lucy lives about forty-five minutes west of St. Louis. Which, for one thing, that's not exactly the rural farmlands, right? And, also, it's been a while since I took social studies, but is Missouri even a prairie state?"

"She's a fraud," Frank said happily. "A fraudulent butter-churning bitch."

That was three months ago, and since then, without really meaning to, Kirsten has become close friends with Frank. The reassuring part is that, if anything, he monitors Lucy's activities more avidly than Kirsten does—surely his avidity has egged on her own—and Lucy is the subject of 90 percent of all discussions between them. The unsettling part is that Frank also follows several other celebrities as enthusiastically yet spitefully; Kirsten isn't sure where he finds the time.

When Kirsten arrives at work twenty-five minutes late, Frank appears on the threshold of her office and gleefully whispers, "There. Is. A. Shit. Storm. Brewing."

Calmly, Kirsten says, "Oh?" This is the way Frank greets her approximately twice a week. But it turns out that a shit storm *is* brewing: Someone on Kirsten's team stored sample data, data belonging to a national courier company, in the area of the server where production can access it, even though the agreement with the courier company hasn't yet been formalized. Their boss, Sheila, is trying to figure out who messed up, whether anyone from production has used the data, and, if so, how to remove it.

As Kirsten steels herself to speak with Sheila, Frank, who is still standing there, says, "Has your copy of your girlfriend's book arrived?"

"I didn't preorder it. I'm stopping at the store on the way home."

"Well, as soon as you finish, give it to me. Because I am not putting *one penny* in the coffers of that whore."

"Yeah, so you've said." Kirsten squeezes past him.

She definitely isn't the one who failed to sequester the sample data, but it's unclear if Sheila believes her. They have a forty-minute conversation that contains about two minutes' worth of relevant information and instruction and thirty-eight minutes of Sheila venting about how at best they've embarrassed themselves and at worst they're facing a copyright lawsuit. When Kirsten has a chance to check Lucy's various social media accounts, she finds that they're all filled with book promotions. On Twitter and elsewhere is a selfie of Lucy and the host of *The Mariana Show* in the greenroom; their heads are pressed together, and they're beaming.

After two meetings and a conference call, Kirsten gets lunch from a sandwich place around the corner, and it's while she's waiting in line for turkey and Swiss cheese on multigrain bread that she receives Frank's text: a screenshot from the website of a weekly celebrity magazine, with the headline PRAIRIE WIFE COMES OUT AS BISEXUAL. The first one and a half sentences of the article, which are all that's visible, read, "Sources confirm that cookbook writer and television personality Lucy Headrick, known to fans as the Prairie Wife, revealed during today's taping of *The Mariana Show* that she has dated multiple women. The married mother of three, who—"

Another text arrives from Frank. It reads, "OMFG!"

Back in the office, Frank says, "Do you think she mentioned you?"

"No," Kirsten says, though, since receiving Frank's texts, she has felt very weird, almost nauseated.

"What if she's carried a torch for you all this time and she looks directly at the camera and says, 'Kirsten, please make haste to my quaint rural farmstead, pull off my muslin knickers, and lick my evangelical pussy'?"

"Jesus, Frank," Kirsten says. "Not like there's anything private about what I told you."

Her phone rings, and she can see on the caller ID that it's Casey. To Frank, she says, "I need to answer this."

"Ian has strings practice after school, and he forgot his violin," Casey says. "I know this is annoying, but could you get it? I have a meeting with the superintendent."

"I don't think I can," Kirsten says. "Sheila's in a really bad mood today. Anyway, maybe Ian should deal with the consequences. You want him to develop grit, right?"

"You think he should just sit there while everyone else practices?"

"I can imagine more traumatizing childhood experiences." Kirsten is, nevertheless, about to relent when Casey says, "God damn it, Kirsten."

"I thought we didn't swear anymore," Kirsten says. There's a silence, and she asks, "Did you just hang up on me?"

"No," Casey says. "But I need to prepare for my meeting. I'll see you at home."

Which, if either of them, is delivering the violin? This is how Casey wins, Kirsten thinks—by *not* insisting on resolution, which compels Kirsten toward it. On a regular basis, Kirsten wonders if Casey is using middle school pedagogical techniques on her.

She stews for the next ninety minutes, until she has to go home and get the violin or it will be too late; then she stands and grabs her purse. Like an apparition, Frank is back in her office.

He says, "If we leave now, we can go to Flanagan's and watch Lucy on *Mariana*. And I do mean *on*."

"I'm sure it'll be online later today."

"Don't you want to know if she mentions you?"

Kirsten hesitates, then says, "Fuck it. I'll come with you."

"For realsies? What were you about to do instead?"

Kirsten sighs. "Good question."

It is seven minutes to three when Kirsten and Frank enter Flanagan's Ale House. Four other patrons are there, two old men sitting side by side at the bar and two younger men sitting by themselves at separate tables.

Frank gestures toward the TV above the bar and says to the bartender, "Can you change the channel to *The Mariana Show*?"

"We'll buy drinks," Kirsten adds. But then the thought of returning to the office with beer on her breath makes her wonder if Sheila will fire her, and she orders seltzer water and French fries; Frank asks for a gin and tonic, and when their drinks are in front of them, he clinks his glass against hers and says, "To lesbians."

Kirsten has only ever seen clips of *The Mariana Show,* and it turns out that there's a lot to get through before Lucy appears—Mariana's monologue, then a trivia contest among audience members, then a filmed segment in which Mariana takes a belly-dancing class. Plus endless commercials. As the minutes tick by, the afternoon is drained of its caperlike mood. She and Frank speak intermittently. She says, "I don't think she *could* mention me, even if she wanted to. Like, from a legal perspective, since I'm a private citizen. And I'm sure she was involved with other girls."

Finally, after more commercials, Mariana introduces Lucy, and Lucy walks out to energetic cheering and applause. She sits on a purple armchair next to Mariana's purple armchair, and the cover of *Dishin' with the Prairie Wife* is projected onto an enormous screen behind them.

Lucy looks great—she's wearing a short-sleeved, belted blue dress with a pattern of roses—and she's also palpably nervous in a way that Kirsten finds surprisingly sympathetic. Lucy is smiling a lot, but she keeps widening her eyes in an oddly alert way, and she appears to be shaking.

Lucy and Mariana discuss a recipe in the memoir for raccoon stew; Lucy says that she personally isn't crazy about it but that it was given to her by her mother-in-law.

"You weren't raised on a farm," Mariana says.

"I wasn't," Lucy says. "I grew up in the suburbs of Phoenix. My dad was an engineer, and my mom was a teacher." Her matter-of-factness also elicits Kirsten's sympathy. Even if her fame is country-fried, even if she speaks in a nebulous drawl, Kirsten cannot remember ever seeing Lucy lie outright. "A few years after college,

I enrolled in social-work school at the University of Missouri," Lucy continues. "It was while I was doing fieldwork way out in the country that I met my husband. And that was it for both of us. I never expected to fall in love with a farmer, and he never expected to fall in love with a food blogger."

As the image on the screen behind them changes from the book cover to a photograph of Lucy and a handsome man wearing a checked shirt and a cowboy hat, Mariana says, "Something in your book—and it's a fantastic read—but something that surprised me is that before you got married to the Stud in Overalls, as we fondly refer to him, you dated women."

Lucy nods and says, both matter-of-factly and shakily, "I did, in my late teens and early twenties. I consider myself bisexual."

"Oh yeah, you do, bitch," Frank says. "Booyah!"

"Can you not talk over her?" Kirsten says.

Mariana, who Kirsten hopes is feigning naïveté for her viewers, says, "But if you're married to a man, you're not still bisexual, are you?"

"Well, my husband and I are monogamous, but I think even if your circumstances change, your core identity remains. Like, heaven forbid, if my husband passed away, I'd still be madly in love with him."

Really? Kirsten thinks. *Madly?*

Mariana asks, "Do you worry about how your fans will react to this news?"

"I love my fans," Lucy says, and turns and waves at the studio audience, which explodes in applause. Though, surely, an audience in Southern California is not representative of Lucy's base.

Over the cheering, Mariana says, "This is just a hunch, but it seems like they love you, too." More thunderous cheering ensues.

"Really," Lucy says. "I gave this serious thought. I prayed on it, I talked to my preacher, I talked to my family. And obviously things are a lot better now for the LGBT community than they once were, but you still hear about teenagers taking their lives, or being made to feel like they're less than. So I decided to let them know, Hey, you're not alone."

Kirsten thinks of Lucy at the camp-counselor orientation in 1994, and then she thinks, What if Lucy *isn't* a greedy, phony hypocrite? What if she's still herself, as surprised by the turns her life has taken as Kirsten sometimes is by hers? In Flanagan's, it occurs to Kirsten that she might be witnessing a genuinely important cultural moment, which makes her wish that she were with someone other than Frank.

"I'm so verklempt," he says. "I need a hug." She assumes he's being sarcastic, but when she glances at him, he's teared up for real. He makes a sheepish expression and says, in a thick, wet voice, "I can't believe your girlfriend is ruining my mascara."

What choice does she have? In her arms, he smells like gin and some leathery cologne, and she's still holding him when he lets loose with a huge, guttural sob.

"Oh, Frank," Kirsten says.

After she leaves work, Kirsten doesn't stop to buy Lucy's book. When she arrives home, the boys greet her at the front door.

"Mama, how many tickles do you need to make an octopus laugh?" Jack says.

"I don't know, how many?"

"I forgot my violin, but Mom brought it to me," Ian says.

"I hope you thanked her," Kirsten says.

"You need ten tickles," Jack says.

In the kitchen, Casey is dumping mayonnaise into a large clear bowl, onto chunks of canned tuna.

"Melts?" Kirsten says by way of greeting, and Casey nods. As Kirsten washes her hands, Casey says, "Will you pull out the salad ingredients? There's a yellow pepper."

"I appreciate your getting Ian's violin."

"We need to be better organized in the morning," Casey says. "I'm setting my alarm for fifteen minutes earlier tomorrow."

"Okay." After a pause, Kirsten says, "Did you hear that Lucy Headrick came out on *The Mariana Show*? Or whatever coming out is called if it's retroactive."

"Who's Lucy Headrick again?"

Oh, to be Casey! Calm and methodical, with a do-gooder job. To be a person who isn't frittering away her life having vengeful thoughts about people from her past! It happens that Casey is both a former farm girl, of the authentic kind—she grew up in Flandreau, South Dakota—and a gold-star lesbian. She and Kirsten met thirteen years ago, at the Christmas-caroling party of a mutual friend. Kirsten got very drunk and climbed onto Casey's lap during "Good King Wenceslas," and that night she stayed over at Casey's apartment.

"Lucy Headrick is the Prairie Wife," Kirsten says. "She just wrote a book."

"Got it," Casey says.

"She was actually very eloquent. And her fans are definitely the kind of people who are still bigots."

"Good for her."

"Are you pissed at me?"

"No," Casey says. "But I'm trying to get dinner on the table."

Kirsten puts the boys to bed, then lies down in the master bedroom and looks at her phone. It's difficult to estimate what portion of the tweets Lucy has received this afternoon are ugly—they're mixed in with "Yay for standing your truth Lucy!" and "I love you no matter what!!!" Maybe a third?

"why u like to eat pussy did u ever try a hard cock"

"You are A LESBIAN ADULTERER. You are DISGUSTING + BAD for AMERICA!!!!!"

"Romans 1:26 two women is ' against nature' "

Quickly, before she can talk herself out of it, Kirsten types, "I thought you were very brave today." After hitting Tweet, she feels a surge of adrenaline and considers deleting the message, but for whose benefit? Her three bots? In any case, Lucy hasn't tweeted since before noon, and Kirsten wonders if she's gone on a Twitter hiatus.

In the summer, Kirsten and Casey usually watch TV together after the boys are asleep, but during the school year Casey works in the den—responding to parents' emails, reading books about how educators can recognize multiple kinds of intelligence. Sometimes she keeps a baseball or a football game on mute, and the sports further deter Kirsten from joining her. Thus, almost every night, Kirsten stays upstairs, intending to fold laundry or call her mother while actually fucking around on her phone. At 9:45, she texts Casey, "Going to bed," and Casey texts back, "Gnight hon," followed by a sleeping-face emoji with "zzz" above the closed eyes. This is their nightly exchange, and every night, for about four seconds, Kirsten ponders Casey's choice of the sleeping-face emoji versus something more affectionate, like the face blowing a kiss, or just a heart.

While brushing her teeth, Kirsten receives a text from Frank: "Bitch did u see this?" There's a link to what she's pretty sure is a Prairie Wife article, and she neither clicks on it nor replies.

She is still awake, in the dark, when Casey comes upstairs almost an hour later, uses the bathroom, and climbs into bed without turning on the light; Kirsten rarely speaks to Casey at this juncture and always assumes that Casey thinks she's asleep. But tonight, while curled on her side with her back to Casey, Kirsten says, "Did you sign Ian's permission slip for the field trip to the science museum?"

"Yeah, it was due last Friday."

"Oh," Kirsten says. "Imagine that."

They're both quiet as Casey settles under the blankets, then she says, "Did the prairie lady mention you on TV?"

"I probably would have told you if she had."

"Good point." Unexpectedly, Casey leans over and kisses Kirsten's cheek. She says, "Well, no matter what, I owe her a debt of gratitude for initiating you."

For some reason, Kirsten tears up. She swallows, so

that she won't sound as if she's crying, and says, "Do you really feel that way, or are you joking?"

"Do you think you'd have dated women if she hadn't hit on you behind the arts-and-crafts shed?"

"And your life is better because you ended up with me?"

Casey laughs. "Who else would I have ended up with?"

"Lots of people. Someone less flaky and petty."

"I like your flakiness and pettiness."

Kirsten starts crying harder, though still not as hard as Frank was crying at the bar. But enough that Casey becomes aware of it and scoots toward her, spooning her from behind.

"Baby," Casey says. "Why are you sad?"

"This will sound self-centered," Kirsten says. "But Lucy was really into me. I'm sure it was partly because I wasn't that into her, and I wasn't even playing hard to get. I just—" She pauses.

"What?" Casey says.

"I know we have a good life," Kirsten says. "And the boys—they're amazing. They amaze me every day. Did I tell you, when we were at the mall last weekend, Jack wanted to buy you this purse that was like a fake-diamond-encrusted jaguar head? Its eyes were emeralds."

"Oh, man," Casey says. "I can't wait for my birthday."

"It's not that I'm jealous of Lucy Headrick because she's a rich celebrity," Kirsten says. "It seems awful to be famous now." Her voice breaks as she adds, "I just wish that there was someone who was excited about me. Or that when someone *was* excited about me, I wish I hadn't taken it for granted. I didn't understand that that would be the only time."

"Kirsten." Casey uses her top hand to pet Kirsten's hip.

"I don't blame you for not finding me exciting," Kirsten says. "Why would you?"

"We have full-time jobs and young kids," Casey says. "This is what this stage is like."

"But do you ever feel like you'll spend every day slicing cucumbers for lunch boxes and going to work and driving to Little League on the weekend and then you'll look up and twenty years will have passed?"

"God willing," Casey says. She moves both her arms up so she's cupping Kirsten's breasts over her pajama top. "Do you want me to pretend to be Lucy at camp? Or Lucy now? Do you want me to make you a chocolate soufflé?"

"Soufflé is too French," Kirsten says. "Lucy would make apple pie."

They're both quiet, and, weirdly, this is where the conversation ends, or maybe, given that it's past eleven and Casey's alarm is set for six-fifteen or possibly for six, it isn't weird at all. They don't have sex. They don't reach any resolutions. But, for the first time in a while, Kirsten falls asleep with her wife's arms around her.

In the middle of the night, because she can't help herself, Kirsten checks to see if Lucy has responded to her tweet; so far, there's nothing.

Volunteers Are Shining Stars

When I started out volunteering on Monday nights at New Day House, it was just me, Karen, and a rotating cast of eight or ten kids who, with their sticky marker-covered hands and mysteriously damp clothes, would greet us by lunging into our arms and leading us into the basement playroom. Karen was a tall, thin black woman in her early forties who had a loud laugh and worked as a lobbyist on Capitol Hill. She once told me that she was the oldest of five sisters raised on a farm in North Carolina, and I think this upbringing contributed to her laid-back attitude as a volunteer. Karen and I had basically the same philosophy toward the kids, which was *We'll try to entertain you, but we won't give in to your every whim, and if you're the type to sit by yourself, chewing on a plastic frog in the corner, we'll let you hang out and chew as long as it doesn't look like you're about to cause yourself harm.* For over ten months, before I did the thing I shouldn't have done, Karen and the kids and I existed in a kind of raucous harmony. It was the beginning of June when the third volunteer showed up.

As I punched in the code that unlocked the front door, I could see a white woman on the bench in the entry hall, and I knew immediately that she was the new volunteer. Because of her professional clothes—black pants and a yellow silk blouse—she clearly wasn't one of the mothers, and because she was just sitting there, she clearly wasn't a shelter employee. Once inside, I saw that she had bad skin, which she'd covered in a pale concealer, making it uniform in tone but still bumpy, and shoulder-length wavy brown hair that was dry in that way that means you're too old to wear it long. She was probably about Karen's age.

When we made eye contact, she smiled in an eager, nervous, closed-lipped way, and I offered a closed-lipped smile in return. I sat on the other end of the bench, as far from her as possible. From the dining room, I could hear the clink and clatter of silverware and dishes, and a baby wailing. The families ate dinner at five-thirty, and we came at six, to give the mothers a break. That was the point of volunteers.

At five before six, Na'Shell and Tasaundra sprinted into the hall and hurled themselves onto my lap. Just behind them was Tasaundra's younger brother, Dewey, who was two and walked in a staggering way. Behind him was another boy who had been there for the first time the week before, whose name I couldn't remember—he looked about four and had tiny gold studs in both ears. He stood by the pay phone, watching us, and I waved and said, "Hey there."

"I'm braiding your hair," Tasaundra announced. She

had already wedged herself behind me and was easing the elastic band out of my ponytail.

"Can I braid your hair, too?" Na'Shell said. "Miss Volunteer, I want to do your hair." Both of them were five. Once Tasaundra had asked me, "Can you do this?" and jumped three times. I had jumped just as she had, at which point she'd grinned, pointed at me with her index finger, and said, "Your boobies is *bouncin'*." Then she and Na'Shell had shrieked with laughter.

The woman on the other side of the bench said, "Oh!"

I turned.

"I heard them call you—you must be—I'm just starting—" She giggled a little.

"I'm Frances," I said.

"Alaina." She stuck out her hand, but I motioned with my chin down to my own right hand, which Na'Shell was gripping. The truth is that if my hand hadn't been occupied, I still wouldn't have wanted to shake Alaina's. I had a thing then about touching certain people, about dirtiness, and I didn't like Alaina's hair and skin. Strangely, being groped by the kids didn't bother me; there was a purity to their dirtiness because they were so young. But if, say, I was on a crowded elevator and a woman in a tank top was standing next to me and the top of her arm was pressed to the top of mine—if, especially, it was skin on skin instead of skin on clothes—I would feel so trapped and accosted that I'd want to cry.

"They sure like you, don't they?" Alaina said, and she giggled again.

"Did you guys hear that?" I said. "You sure like me, right?"

Na'Shell squealed noncommittally. Alaina would fig-

ure out soon enough how generous the children were
with their affection and also how quickly they'd turn on
you, deciding you had let them down or hurt their feelings. None of it meant much. You tried to show them a
good time for two hours once a week and not to become
attached, because they left without warning. One Monday, a kid was there, and the next, he wasn't—his mom
had found a place for them to live, with her sister or her
mother or her ex-boyfriend or as part of some new program where her own place was subsidized. The longest
the families ever stayed at the shelter was six months, but
most of them were gone far sooner.

Mikhail and Orlean walked through the doorway from
the dining room. At nine and ten, they were the oldest;
boys older than twelve weren't allowed in the shelter because in the past, they'd gotten involved with some of
the younger mothers. "Can we go downstairs now?"
Mikhail asked. Mikhail's two front teeth pointed in opposite directions, so that two-thirds of a triangle formed
in the space where they weren't. In idle moments, he had
a habit of twisting his tongue sideways and poking it
through the triangle.

I looked at my watch. "It's not quite six."

"But there's two of yous."

If we had been in the basement, I'd have said, *Two of
you*. But I never corrected their grammar upstairs, where
the mothers might overhear. I said to Alaina, "The rule is
that two volunteers have to be present before we go
downstairs. You've been through the training, right?"

"I'm ready to dive in headfirst." She actually extended
her arms in front of her head.

I walked to the threshold of the dining room, where

the air smelled like steamed vegetables and fish. Scattered around the tables were a few mothers and a few babies— the babies didn't go to the playroom—and about five more children I recognized. "We're going downstairs," I called. "So if you guys want to—"

"Miss Volunteer!" cried out Derek, and he stood as if to run toward me before his mother pulled him back by one strap of his overalls.

"Boy, you need to finish your dinner," she snapped, and Derek burst into tears. Derek was my favorite: He was three years old and had beautiful long eyelashes and glittering alert eyes and pale brown skin—his mother was white, so I assumed his father was black—and when Derek laughed, his smile was enormous and his laughter was noisy and hoarse. He was the only one I had ever fantasized about taking home with me, setting up a cot for him and feeding him milk and animal crackers and buying him hardcover books with bright illustrations of mountaintop castles or sailboats on the ocean at night. Never mind that I had student loans to pay off and was living with a roommate and never mind that Derek already had a mother and that, in fact, she was one of the more intimidating figures at the shelter: She probably weighed three hundred pounds and often wore sweatpants through which you could see the cellulite on her buttocks and the backs of her thighs; she pulled her hair back in a ponytail that looked painfully tight; her teeth were yellow; her expression was unvaryingly sour. It seemed to me miraculous that she had been the one to give birth to Derek.

Seeing him cry, I wanted simultaneously to apologize to his mother and to pull him away from her and up into my arms, to feel his little calves clamped around my waist, his head pressed between my shoulder and jaw. But I merely ducked back into the entry hall.

Downstairs, I asked loudly, "Who wants to draw?"

Several of the kids shouted, "Me!"

"And who wants to play farm animals?" I asked.

Several of the same ones shouted, "Me!"

"I suppose I can be a cow," Alaina said. "Moo!"

"It's not acting like farm animals," I said. "It's playing with them." I gestured toward the shelf where the bin of plastic figures was stored. "Either you could do the farm animals with them and I could do the drawing, or the other way around."

She walked to the shelf and lifted the bin. "Look at all these fabulous creatures!" she exclaimed. "Oh my goodness! There's a horse, and a chicken, and a pig. Will anyone help me play with these, or do I have to play all alone?"

Tasaundra and Na'Shell hurried over. "I'm the baby sheep," Tasaundra said. "Miss Volunteer, do I get to be the baby sheep?"

"You was the baby sheep before," Na'Shell said.

"But I called it."

"But you already was the baby sheep."

"Na'Shell, be the baby chicks," I said while I pulled the markers from the drawer beneath the sink. "There are *two* baby chicks."

"Then I want to be the baby chicks!" Tasaundra yelled.

I passed paper to Mikhail and Orlean and Dewey and to the boy whose name I hadn't been able to remember upstairs but remembered now: It was Meshaun. The paper came from the shelter's administrative office, with graphs on the back, or information about welfare studies from 1994. Everything the kids played with was somehow second-rate—the markers were dried out, the coloring books were already colored in, the wooden puzzles were gnawed on and had pieces missing. When the boys made paper airplanes, you could see the graphs or the typed words where the wings folded up.

"And what have we here?" I heard Alaina say. "If this is a panda bear, we're living on a very unusual farm indeed. And an alligator? My heavens—perhaps the farm has a little bayou in the back."

I feared that if I looked at her, she'd make some conspiratorial gesture, like winking. I wanted to say, *Shut up and play with the kids.*

This was when Karen arrived, holding Derek's hand. "Sorry I'm late." Seeing Alaina, she added, "I'm Karen."

Alaina stood and extended her arm and, unlike me, Karen took it. "I'm Alaina, and I'm finding that this is *quite* the exotic farm here at New Day House."

"Hey, Derek," I said. "Want to come make a picture?"

As I lifted him onto my lap, he reached for the black marker and said, "I'ma draw me a sword." I loved Derek's husky voice, how surprising it was in a child.

The drawing and farm animals lasted for about ten minutes. Then the kids built a walled town out of blocks, then Orlean knocked it over and Na'Shell began crying, then we played "Mother, May I?" until they all started cheating, and then they chased each other around the playroom and shouted and Mikhail flicked the lights on and off, which he or someone else always did whenever things became unbearably exciting. At eight, after we'd cleaned up, Karen and Alaina headed into the hall with most of the kids. I washed my hands while Na'Shell stood by the sink, watching me. She motioned to her elbow. "Why you do it all the way up here?"

"To be thorough," I said. "Do you know what *thorough* means? It means being very careful." When I'd dried my hands and arms with a paper towel, I used my knuckle to flick off the light switches.

Upstairs, the kids had dispersed. Na'Shell's mom, who had a skinny body and skinny eyebrows and pink eye shadow and enormous gold hoop earrings and who looked no older than fifteen, was waiting in the entry hall. I didn't know her name, or the names of any of the mothers. "Come here, baby," she said to Na'Shell. "What you got?" Our last activity of the night had been making paper jewelry, and Na'Shell passed her mother a purple bracelet.

"Good news," Karen said. "Alaina offered us a ride." Unless it was raining, Karen and I walked home together. The shelter was a few blocks east of Dupont Circle— interestingly, the building it occupied was probably worth a fortune—and Karen and I both lived about two miles away, in Cleveland Park.

"I'm fine walking," I said. The thought of being inside Alaina's car was distinctly unappealing. There were probably long, dry hairs on the seats, and old coffee cups with the imprint of her lipstick.

"Don't be a silly goose," Alaina said. "I live in Bethesda, so you're on my way."

I didn't know how to refuse a second time.

Alaina's car was a two-door, and I sat in back. As she pulled out of the parking lot behind the shelter, Karen said, "They're hell-raisers, huh? Have any kids yourself?"

"As a matter of fact, I just went through a divorce," Alaina said. "But we didn't have children, which was probably a blessing in disguise."

I had noticed earlier that Alaina wasn't wearing a wedding ring; it surprised me that she'd ever been married.

"I'm sorry," Karen said.

"I'm taking it day by day—that old cliché. What about you?"

"Card-carrying spinster," Karen said cheerfully.

This was a slightly shocking comment. At the volunteer training almost a year earlier, it had appeared that the majority of people there were unmarried women nearing the age when they'd be too old to have children. This fact was so obvious that it seemed unnecessary to discuss it out loud. Plus, it made me nervous, because was this the time in my own life before I found someone to love and had a family and looked back longingly on my youthful freedom? Or was it the beginning of what my life would be like forever? One of the reasons I liked Karen was that she was the first woman I'd met in my short adulthood who wasn't married but seemed completely unconcerned about it; she was like proof of something.

We were driving north on Connecticut Avenue, and out the window, it was just starting to get dark. Alaina's and Karen's voices were like a discussion between guests on a radio program playing in the background.

"And how about you?" Alaina said.

The car was silent for several seconds before I realized she was talking to me. "I don't have any kids," I said.

"Are you married?"

In the rearview mirror, we made eye contact.

"No," I said.

"Frances is a baby," Karen said. "Guess how old she is."

Alaina furrowed her brow, as if thinking very hard. "Twenty-four?"

"Twenty-three," I said.

Karen turned around. "You're twenty-three? I thought you were twenty-two."

"I was," I said. "But then I had a birthday."

I hadn't been making a joke, but they both laughed.

"Are you getting school credit for being a volunteer?" Alaina asked.

"No, I've graduated."

"Where do you work?"

Normally, I felt flattered when people asked me questions. With Alaina, I was wary of revealing information. I hesitated, then said, "An environmental organization."

"What's it called?"

"It's on M Street."

Alaina laughed again. "Does it have a name?"

"The National Conservancy Group." Before she could ask me another question, I said, "Where do you work?"

"Right now, I'm a free agent. I consult with nonprofits and NGOs on fundraising."

I wondered if this was a euphemism for being unemployed.

"You get to make your own hours, huh?" Karen said. "I envy you."

"It's definitely a perk," Alaina said.

After Alaina had dropped Karen off and I'd climbed into the front seat, I could not help thinking—I was now alone in an enclosed space with Alaina—that perhaps she was genuinely unbalanced. But if she were violent, I thought, she'd be violent in a crazed rather than a criminal way. She wouldn't rob me; she'd do something bizarre and pointless, like cutting off my thumb. Neither of us spoke, and in the silence, I imagined her making some creepy, telling remark: *Do you ever feel like your eyes are really, really itchy and you just want to scrape at them with a fork?*

But when she spoke, what she said was "It's great that you're volunteering at your age. That's really admirable."

I was almost disappointed. "The kids are fun," I said.

"Oh, I just want to gobble them up. You know who's especially sweet is, who's the little boy with the long eyelashes?"

The question made my ears seize up like when you hear an unexpected noise. "You can stop here," I said. "At the corner, by that market." It suddenly seemed imperative that Alaina not know where I lived.

"I'll wait if you're picking up stuff. I remember what it's like to carry groceries on foot."

"My apartment isn't far," I said. She hadn't yet come to a complete stop, but I'd opened the door and had one leg hanging out. "Thanks for the ride," I added, and slammed the door.

Without turning around, I could tell that she had not yet driven off. *Go,* I thought. *Get out of here.* What was she waiting for? The market door opened automatically, and just before it shut behind me, I finally heard her pull away. For a few minutes, I peered at the street, making sure she didn't pass by again. Then I walked out empty-handed.

———

I'd majored in political science at the University of Kansas and spent the summer after my junior year interning for the congressman from the district in Wichita where I'd grown up. I hadn't socialized much with the other interns, but I'd liked D.C. enough that I'd returned after graduating; the brick rowhouses reminded me of a city in a movie, and even though this was the late nineties, when crime rates were a lot higher than they are now, it didn't *feel* unsafe.

In fact, my postgraduation life bore little resemblance to a movie. During the week, I was often so tired after work that I'd go to bed by eight-thirty. Then on Saturdays and Sundays, I'd hurry up and down Connecticut Avenue, to the laundromat and the market and CVS; because I didn't have a car, I'd load groceries into my backpack, and it would be so heavy that it would make my shoulders ache. Sometimes I'd pass couples eating brunch at the outdoor cafés or inside restaurants with doors that opened onto the sidewalk, and I'd feel a confusion bordering on hostility. Flirting with a guy in a dark bar, at night, when you'd both been drinking—I understood the enticement. But to sit across the table from each other in the daylight, to watch each other's jaws working over pancakes and scrambled eggs, seemed embarrassing and impossible. The compromises you'd made would be so apparent, I thought, this other person before you with their patches of flaky skin and protruding nose hairs and the drop of syrup on their chin before they wiped it and the boring cheerful complaints you'd make to each other about traffic or current events while the horrible sun hung over you. Wouldn't you rather be alone, so you could go back to your apartment and use the toilet, or take a nap without someone's sweaty arm around you? Or maybe you'd just want to sit on your couch and balance your checkbook and not hear another person breathing while they read the newspaper five feet away and looked over every ten or fifteen minutes so that you had to smile back—about nothing!—and periodically utter a term of endearment.

As I ran errands, I'd wear soccer shorts from high school and T-shirts that I'd have perspired through in the back; passing by the cafés, I'd feel hulking and monstrous, and sometimes, to calm down, I would count. I always started with my right hand, one number for each finger except my pinkie: thumb, *one;* index finger, *two;* middle finger, *three;* third finger, *four.* Then I'd go to the left hand, then back to the right. I knew this wasn't the most normal thing in the world, but I thought the fact that I didn't count high was a good sign. I might have worried for myself if I'd reached double or triple digits, but staying under five felt manageable. Anyway, counting was like hiccups; after a few blocks, I'd realize that while I'd been thinking of something else, the impulse had gone away.

The following week, as soon as I entered the shelter, Alaina jumped up from the hall bench holding a grocery bag and, offering each item for my inspection, withdrew a box of markers, a packet of construction paper, two vials of glitter, a tube of glue, and a carton of tiny American flags whose poles were toothpicks. "The kids can make Uncle Sam hats," she said. "For the Fourth of July."

In the last week, I had decided that my initial reaction

to Alaina had been unfair; she hadn't done anything truly strange or offensive. But in her presence again, I was immediately reminded of a hyper, panting dog with bad breath.

"Then we'll have a parade," she continued. "You know, get in the spirit."

"We're not allowed to take the kids outside." Not only that, but if our paths crossed with theirs in the world—if, say, I saw Tasaundra and her mother at the Judiciary Square Metro stop—I was not even supposed to speak to them. I also wasn't supposed to learn their last names.

"Inside, then," Alaina said. "We'll have the first annual super-duper New Day House indoor parade. And for next week I was thinking we could do dress-up. I found some of my bridesmaid dresses that I'm sure Tasaundra and Na'Shell would think are to die for. So when you go home, look in your closet and see what you have— graduation gowns, Halloween costumes."

I thought of my half-empty closet. Unlike Alaina, apparently, I actually wore all my clothes.

I then watched as she walked into the dining room and said, in a loud, fake-forlorn voice, "I can't find anyone to play with. Are there any fun boys or girls in here who'll be my friends?"

I imagined the mothers scowling at her, though what I heard were the screams of the kids, followed by the squeaks and thuds of their feet as they hurried across the linoleum floor. I wondered if Alaina thought that winning them over so quickly was an achievement.

In the basement—Karen arrived shortly after we'd gone down—the hat-making occurred with a few hitches, most notably when Na'Shell spilled the red glitter on the floor, then wept, but it didn't go as badly as I'd hoped. "Great idea, Alaina," Karen said.

Alaina stood. "Okay, everyone," she said. "Parade time." She set a cylinder of blue construction paper on top of her head—of course she had made one for herself. "Do I look *exactly* like Lady Liberty?"

The kids regarded her blankly. But pretty soon, they'd all lined up. As we left the playroom—I was in the middle, holding Derek's hand—I heard singing. It was Alaina, I realized, and the song was "America the Beautiful." And she was really belting it out. Had I only imagined her jittery, inhibited persona from the week before?

We cut through the dining room, where the only person present was Svetlana, the shelter employee on duty Monday night. She was sitting at a table filling out a form, and she blinked at us as we walked around the periphery of the room. By then, Alaina was singing "The Star-Spangled Banner" and Mikhail was blowing a kazoo whose origins I was unsure of. From behind her, I looked at Alaina's awful hair, her cotton sleeveless sweater, which was cream-colored and cabled, and her dry and undefined upper arms.

Back in the stairwell, I saw that Alaina was going up.

"Hey," I said.

She didn't stop.

"Hey."

She looked at me over one shoulder.

"Those are the bedrooms," I said.

"So?"

"I think we should respect their privacy."

"But look how cute the kids are." Alaina leaned over and cupped Derek's chin with one hand. "What a hand-

some boy you are, Derek," she crooned. She straight-
ened up and said to me, "I'm sure it's fine."

I looked at her face, and I could see that this wasn't
about challenging me, that, in fact, I had nothing to do
with it. This really was about the parade; something in
the situation had made her giddy in a way I myself had
never, ever been—utterly unself-conscious and eager.
Her chest rose and fell as if she'd been exercising, she was
panting a little, and as she smiled, I could see her big
front teeth and gums, I could see the mustache of pale
hairs above her lip, her uneven skin, her bright and happy
eyes. She was experiencing a moment of profound personal triumph, though nothing was occurring that was
remotely profound or triumphant. It was a Monday evening; these were children; and really, underneath it all,
weren't we just killing time, didn't none of it matter?

"Karen, don't you feel like we should stay down here?"
I said.

"Ehh—I don't think anyone would mind."

I stared between them. I had felt certain that Karen
would agree with me.

"Don't worry so much." Alaina punched my shoulder. "It'll give you wrinkles."

The second floor was a corridor with two rooms on
either side, like a dorm, but none of the rooms had doors.
Inside were bunk beds, as many as four in a row; I knew
they made the families double up. The first room on the
right was empty. I glanced through the doorway on the
left and saw Mikhail's mother hunched on a bottom bunk,
painting her nails, her infant daughter lying next to her. I
wondered if the nail polish fumes were bad for the baby,
and as I was wondering this, my eyes met Mikhail's moth-

er's. Her mouth was pursed contemptuously, and her eyebrows were raised, as if she'd sensed me judging her.

In the second room on the left, two mothers were sleeping. As I passed that doorway, continuing to follow Alaina, who was still singing, and Mikhail, who was still playing the kazoo, one of the mothers rolled over, and I hurried by—let her see someone else when she looked for who'd awakened her. In the last room on the right, Alaina found her audience. She knocked ceremoniously on the doorframe.

"Excuse me, ladies," she said. "I have with me a group of patriots eager to show you their artistic creations. Will you permit us to enter?"

After a pause, one woman said, "You want to, you can come in."

We filed into the room—there were so many of us that Karen had to remain in the hall—and I saw that Derek's mother and Orlean's mother were sitting on the floor with a basket of laundry between them and piles of folded clothes set in stacks on a lower bunk.

Derek yelled, "Mama!" and tumbled into her lap.

"Would someone like to say the Pledge of Allegiance?" Alaina looked around at the children. "Who knows it? 'I pledge allegiance to the flag . . .'"

"'. . . of the United States of America,'" Orlean said, but then he didn't continue; only Alaina did.

It was excruciating. When she got to the end, the room was silent, and I couldn't look at the mothers. How loud and earnest we must have seemed to them, how repugnantly bourgeois, clutching at their children. I started clapping, because I didn't know what else to do, and then the kids clapped, too.

It wasn't just that the mothers intimidated me; they also made me jealous. I'd once heard Tasaundra and Dewey's mother having an argument on the pay phone about buying diapers, and as she yelled and cursed, I couldn't help but be impressed by her sheer forcefulness. The mothers' lives were complicated. And by definition, they all had children, who had come from having sex. Even when they lived in New Day, a place where men were prohibited from entering, romantic entanglements found these women: problems they thought about hard while sitting on the front steps, smoking. Other people were so unsuccessful in fending off love! Members of Congress who had affairs with their aides, or students I'd known in college, girls who as freshmen declared themselves lesbians, then graduated with boyfriends—to give in to such love represented, for them, a capitulation or a betrayal, yet apparently the pull was so strong that they couldn't resist. That was what I didn't understand, how people made the leap from not mattering in each other's lives to mattering.

Another thing that impressed me about the mothers was their sexiness. Derek's mother wore sweatpants and T-shirts, but some of the others, whether or not they were overweight, dressed in tight, revealing clothes, and they looked good: tank tops and short skirts, no stockings and heeled mules, gold necklaces and bracelets and rings.

Back in the playroom, Alaina beamed and giggled, and I could tell that she considered the parade an unqualified success. "Frances, are you always such a stickler for the rules?" she asked in a teasing voice.

"I guess I am." Though what happened later might

make this a dubious claim, I already knew that it wasn't worth it to have conflicts with people you weren't invested in.

"No hard feelings, right?" Alaina said. "It seemed like the moms were totally psyched to have us come through."

I said nothing, and turned away from her.

At the end of the night, Derek waited with me when the others went upstairs, and Alaina said, "I'll get the lights. You can go up."

"That's okay," I said. "I'm usually the one to stay behind."

"All the more reason for you to go up." Her tone was friendly, like she was doing me a favor.

"Actually," I said, "I prefer to stay." I was standing by the sink, and I turned on the water.

"You always wash your hands, huh?" Alaina said.

"Gotta watch out for cooties," I said. "Ready, Derek?"

"I've noticed that about you, how much you wash your hands," Alaina said.

I turned and looked at her, and I could feel that my mouth was a hard line. "You're very observant," I said. She took a step back. I said, "Derek, do you want to turn off the lights?"

Normally, I wouldn't have picked up a child after washing my hands, but I liked Derek so much that it was a kind of visceral distraction; plus, it was a way of proving Alaina wrong. Besides, I told myself, I could stop on the way home to wash my hands again at a café on Eighteenth Street.

I carried Derek to the light switches, and he turned them off. On the other side of the door, I set him down. He took my hand, and though my entire body was tense from the exchange with Alaina, I felt some of Derek's placidity, his sweetness, seep into me. Alaina reached for his other hand.

"Oh my," she said. "What have we here?"

"No!" Derek said. "It's mine."

I glanced down and saw that Alaina was extracting from his grip one of the piglets from the farm animals bin.

"That's not yours," Alaina said. "That belongs to all the children at New Day. Look." She held the piglet toward me. It had peach skin and pink hooves and a little curly tail, and its snout pointed skyward. "Frances, don't you think if he took this pig, the other kids would feel really sad?"

I said, through clenched teeth, "Let him have it."

"Doesn't that send a confusing message?" Her voice was normal, no longer singsongy for Derek.

"It's a plastic pig," I said. "He's three." I thought of the objects I had coveted as a child: an eraser in the shape of a strawberry that belonged to Deanna Miller, the girl who sat next to me in first grade; a miniature perfume bottle of my mother's with a round top of frosted glass. My mother had promised that she would give me the bottle when she was finished with the perfume, but year after year, a little of the amber liquid always remained. There weren't that many times in your life when you believed a possession would bring you happiness and you were actually right.

"You know what I'll do, Derek?" Alaina said. "I'll put the pig back, but when you come down here tomorrow, you'll know just where it is."

I knew she would think we'd compromised, but she

could compromise by herself. While she was in the play-room, I lifted Derek again and carried him upstairs.

I kept waiting that week to get a call from Linda, the New Day director, saying she'd received complaints from the mothers about our excursion to the second floor. I would apologize and take responsibility for my participation in the parade, but I'd also explain that Alaina was the one who had initiated it and that, in general, I had concerns about her behavior as a volunteer; while eating my dinner of microwaved cheese quesadillas at night, I rehearsed the way I'd phrase this. But the week passed without a call.

The next Monday was quiet. Orlean had, to the envy of everyone, gone out for pizza with his father, and Tasaun-dra and Dewey and their mom had moved out of the shelter to stay with a cousin in Prince George's County. A new girl named Marcella was there, a chubby, dreamy eight-year-old with long black hair.

Alaina's dress-up clothes went over well enough, ex-cept that the entire process, from the kids' choosing what to wear to putting on the outfits to taking the clothes back off again, took less than fifteen minutes. Alaina en-couraged the kids to draw pictures of themselves in the clothes, but all anybody wanted to play was "Mother, May I?" I wondered if Alaina would keep hatching schemes week after week or if she would soon realize that with kids, you didn't get points just for trying.

While I was putting together a wooden puzzle of the United States with Marcella and Meshaun, Derek came over to the table. He said, "Miss Volunteer," and when I said, "Yes, Derek?" he giggled and ran behind my chair.

I whirled around, and Derek shrieked. He tossed something into the air, and when it landed on the floor, I saw that it was the pig from the week before. He picked it up and made it walk up my arm.

Alaina squatted by Derek. "Do you like your pig?" she asked.

I couldn't help myself. "*His* pig?"

But I noticed that Alaina was fighting a smile the way people do when they've received a compliment and want you to think they don't believe it. "It is his," she said. "I gave it to him."

Then I saw that the pig wasn't identical to the one from before—this pig's snout was pointed straight in front of it, and its skin was more pink than peach.

"I felt like such a witch taking the other one away," she said.

I stared at her. "When did you give it to him?"

"I came by last week."

Knowing that she had been at the shelter at a time other than Monday evening made me curious about what Linda had made of that, or whether Alaina had met other volunteers. And had Alaina summoned Derek in order to give him the pig in private, or had she handed it over in front of other children? She should be fired, I thought, if it was possible to fire a volunteer.

That night as we left the shelter, Alaina said, "Anyone up for a drink?"

"Sounds good to me," Karen said.

"I need to be at work early tomorrow," I said. Karen and I had never socialized outside the shelter.

"You know, Frances, I looked at the National Con-servancy Group's website the other day," Alaina said. "I know your president from back in the day. David, right?"

"I don't really work with him directly," I said. "I'm entry-level."

Alaina elbowed me. "No low self-esteem, you hear? You're just starting out. Listen—I'm impressed that you landed a job at such a great place."

I offered her my closed-lipped smile.

"Karen," Alaina said, "do we have to forcibly drag this girl out for one lousy Budweiser?"

"At her age, she should be dragging us," Karen said.

"I really can't," I said. "Sorry."

As I walked away, Alaina called, "Hey, Frances," and when I turned back, she said, "Bye, Miss Volunteer." Her voice contained a performative note that made me suspect she'd thought up the farewell ahead of time and saved it, for just this moment, to say aloud.

I washed my hands and forearms at the café on Eigh-teenth Street, and then, when I got back to my apart-ment, I washed them again and changed out of my street clothes. I knew that I washed my hands a lot—I wasn't an idiot—but it was always for a reason: because I'd come in from outside, because I'd been on the subway or used the toilet or touched money. It wasn't as if, sitting at my desk at the office, I simply jumped up, raced to the bath-room, and began to scrub.

Usually when I got home at night, my roommate, whom I hardly knew, wasn't there. She had a boyfriend, another grad student, and she spent a lot of time at his place. It was mostly on the weekends that I saw them. Sometimes on Saturday mornings when I left to run errands, they'd be entwined on the living room couch, watching television, and when I returned hours later, they'd be in the same position. Once I'd seen him prepare breakfast in bed for her by toasting frozen waffles, then coating them with spray-on olive oil. I was glad on the nights they weren't around. After I was finished washing my hands and changing my clothes, it was like I'd completed everything that was required of me and I could just give in to inertia.

It was storming the next Monday: big, rolling gray clouds split by lightning and followed by cracks of thunder. The director, Linda, was wearing a jacket, peering out the front door, when I arrived. She was often leaving as I was arriving, and she said, "The rush-hour downpour—gotta love it, huh?"

I was the first volunteer there. When the kids came out of the dining room, Meshaun was clutching a red rubber ball and Orlean was attempting to take it away, which made Meshaun howl. As I tried to adjudicate, Derek's mother descended from the second floor and said, "You know where D's at?"

"Sorry, but I just got here," I said.

"Monique told me she'd watch him, and now she don't know where he is."

"Derek's lost?" My heart began beating faster. "If he's lost, you should tell Svetlana."

As Derek's mother walked into the dining room, I

hurried downstairs, but the playroom was silent, and all the lights were off. "Derek?" I called. "Are you here, Derek?" I flicked the lights on and looked under the tables, behind the shelves. But in the silence, I would have been able to hear him breathing.

When I returned upstairs, the hall was crowded with mothers and children, plus Alaina and Karen had both arrived; Alaina was holding a collapsed, dripping umbrella as Svetlana asked when people had last seen Derek. I was glad I hadn't been present when Alaina had learned that he was missing—she'd probably opened her mouth, covered it with her palm, and gasped.

Svetlana, whose apparent lack of panic was both reassuring and unsettling, gestured at me. "Why don't you go outside with Crystal and look?" Crystal, I realized, was the name of Derek's mother.

I still had my raincoat on, and Alaina offered me her umbrella, which I didn't take. Despite the seriousness of the moment, it felt awkward to walk outside with Derek's mother—I wasn't sure if we were supposed to split up or stay together. I glanced at her, and her face was scrunched with anxiety.

"He couldn't have gone far, right?" I said.

"I'm gonna beat his ass," she said, but she sounded frightened.

We did split up—I walked toward one end of the block, calling his name in such a manner that a passerby might have thought I was summoning a puppy. The cars made swishing noises as they passed, and my stomach tightened with each one. The roads had to be slick, and the rain on the windshields would make everything blurry. It was hard to know if it was worse to imagine him alone or with someone—if he was alone, I hoped the thunder and lightning weren't scaring him.

I walked around the side of the shelter, expecting and not expecting to see him. In my mind, he was wearing what he'd been wearing the day Alaina had taken the pig, a red-and-blue-striped T-shirt and black sweatpants. I found his mother standing on her tiptoes, peering into the dumpster in the tiny rear parking lot and shoving aside pieces of cardboard. "You think he could have gotten in there?" I said. She didn't reply, and I added, "You know the new volunteer who has kind of light brown hair? She came here a couple of weeks ago some night besides Monday, right? She brought Derek a little pig?"

"I don't know nothing about that."

"I'm wondering if you've seen her here other times. Has she ever invited Derek to do stuff during the day?"

For the first time, Derek's mother looked at me, and I saw that she was on the verge of crying. She said, "I never should of left D with Monique." Then her face collapsed—big, scary Derek's mother—and as she brought her hands up to shield it, her shoulders shook. What I was supposed to do, what the situation unmistakably called for, was to hug her, or at the very least to set my arm around her back. I couldn't do it. She was wearing an old-looking, off-white T-shirt that said LUCK O' THE IRISH across the chest in puffy green letters, and I just couldn't. If I did, after I got home, even if I changed out of my clothes and showered, her hug would still be on me.

"I'm sorry," I said. "I'm so sorry—I'm—by the way, are you under twenty-four? Because I read about this program where if you are, you can take a class to prepare for the GED and it's subsidized. Maybe that would be a good thing for you and Derek?"

She lifted her head and looked at me, appearing bewildered. In that moment, from inside the dining room, Karen rapped on a closed windowpane and made a thumbs-up gesture. "Oh!" I said. "I think they found him!"

Back inside, the entry hall was still dense with mothers and children, and Derek, before she passed him off to his mother, was in Alaina's arms. On his left cheek was the imprint of a pillow or a wrinkled sheet, and he was yawning without covering his mouth. I heard Alaina say, "And then I just thought, Could that little lump on the top bunk be him? I was on my way out, but something made me check one more time. . . ."

The combination of the accumulated people, the relieved energy, and the storm outside made it seem almost like we were having a party; at any moment, a cake would appear. "You gotta watch your babies like a hawk," someone beside me said, and when I glanced over, I saw that it was Meshaun's mother. Her voice was not disapproving but happy. "Like. A. Hawk," she repeated, nodding her head once for each word.

When we finally took the children down to the playroom, I couldn't shake a feeling of agitation. Alaina held hands in a circle with Na'Shell and Marcella while, in an English accent, singing the *My Fair Lady* song "I Could Have Danced All Night," and if I'd ever hated anyone more, I didn't recall when.

At the end of the hour, I did, for once, let Alaina stay behind and turn off the lights, and as Karen and I climbed the steps with the children, I murmured, "Do you think Alaina could have had something to do with Derek's disappearance? She's kind of obsessed with him."

In a normal-volumed voice, Karen said, "No, she *found* Derek."

"Yeah, supposedly," I said. "But she came here once in the middle of the week just to give him a present. And she showed up late tonight, which she never does." As the children joined their waiting mothers in the entry hall, Karen and I said our goodbyes to them. Then, still speaking under my breath and just to Karen, I said, "Has it ever occurred to you that Alaina might be a little— I don't know—unhinged?"

Karen laughed. "She just marches to the beat of a different drummer."

"She has really bad judgment, like with the parade. She didn't even realize how the mothers reacted."

"I thought the parade was cute."

I tried not to show my surprise. "I don't trust her," I said. "I wouldn't put it past Alaina to have hidden Derek in some closet so she could be the one to find him."

For several seconds, Karen looked at me. But all she said was "I don't think she'd do that."

Then Alaina herself was at the top of the stairs, and as the three of us walked out the front door, she said, "Whew—what a night, huh? I think we all need a drink, and tonight I'm not taking no for an answer, Miss Frances."

"I'm not going out for a drink with you," I said. I looked at Karen as I added, "Bye."

"Frances," Alaina said. "Hold on." We'd reached the bottom of the steps. "If I offended you when I asked about your OCD, I want to apologize."

I stared at her. "Excuse me?"

"I have a cousin who has it, and it doesn't have to be this debilitating thing," Alaina said. "My cousin's on medication, and she's doing real well."

"I'm not obsessive-compulsive," I said. "And it's none of your business."

"Frances, it's okay. I'm not—"

"It's okay?" I said. I could hear my voice growing louder.

"Frances, relax," Karen said.

"*You're* telling *me* it's okay when you're the one who has no grip on reality?" I said to Alaina. "It's obvious that you live in this imaginary world where you believe—you believe—" I paused. Our faces were only a few feet apart, and in the dusk I saw a tiny dot of my spit land on Alaina's jaw. She didn't rub it away; she seemed paralyzed, staring at me with curiosity and confusion. "You believe that people are watching you go through your life," I said. "That if you use a big vocabulary word, someone will be impressed, or if you make a joke, someone will laugh, or that you're scoring points by buying glitter for underprivileged children. But no one cares. Do you understand that? No one gives a shit what you do. And everyone can see how desperate and pathetic you are, so you might as well just stop pretending that you—"

"Whoa there, Frances," Karen said. "Let's all take a deep breath."

"Next time she'll probably kidnap Derek for good," I said. "Then you can tell me to take a deep breath."

I had always respected Karen, but in this moment she seemed dismissive of me because I was young; she seemed fundamentally oblivious. I turned to leave, and Alaina said, "We just want to help you, Frances."

I whirled around. Though this was when I lunged toward Alaina, though I placed my hands on either side of her throat, though I pressed them inward and felt the delicate bones of her neck beneath her warm and grotesque skin, I really didn't mean to hurt her; it's not that I was trying to *strangle* her. Her eyes widened and she was blinking a lot, her eyelids flapping as she brought her own hands up to my wrists to pry my hands away. But that gave me something to resist. I squeezed more tightly, and she made a retching noise.

"Let go of her, Frances," Karen said, and she was tugging on my shoulders. "Let go right now or I'm calling the police."

It actually wasn't the threat so much as the interruption—an outside voice, a third party—that made me drop my grip. I can't say that I ever cared what Alaina thought of me, though I did regret later that Karen had witnessed it. In her eyes, I was probably a person she once knew who turned out to be crazy.

Outside the shelter, Alaina coughed and panted in a way that struck me even then as theatrical. Before I hurried away, I said to her, "You disgust me."

I never went back to the shelter, and I never spoke to any of them again. I received four messages at work from Linda, the shelter's director, all of which I deleted without listening to them.

Around Christmas, I received a donation request from New Day. That I was still on their mailing list was probably, given the circumstances under which I'd stopped volunteering, an oversight. New Day was affiliated with two other shelters on Capitol Hill, and the request came with a calendar that said, on the front, VOLUNTEERS ARE SHINING STARS! For each month, the picture was of kids and adults playing at the various shelters, and Alaina was featured for the month of March. Had she been posing with Derek, the calendar would have felt karmically punitive; in fact, she was doing a puzzle with a boy I'd never seen.

I wondered if any of the children noticed my absence or asked where I'd gone, or if I was just another in a long line of adults who slipped without explanation from their lives. For a while, I contemplated what I'd do if I saw one of them on the street. Because of the shelter rules, it would have to be a subtle gesture, less than a wave, something a mother wouldn't detect—a raise of the eyebrows, a flare of the nostrils, a wiggling pinkie finger. But I moved away from Washington without running into any of them.

It was a Sunday morning about three months after I'd last been to the shelter when I saw Karen. A couple emerged from the bagel place near my apartment holding hands, the guy carrying a brown bag, and I watched them for a moment before I realized the woman was tall, cheerful Karen, the self-declared spinster. Was this a new development? They were talking, and then he turned and kissed her; he was slightly shorter than she was. Before she could notice me, I crossed the street.

Do-Over

Clay never seriously considered the possibility that Donald Trump would win the election, and around nine P.M. central time, when it seems likely he will, Clay texts his daughter, Abby, who is fourteen and at her mother's house. He writes, *I hope you are not too disappointed. Progress sometimes happens in fits and starts. I love you, Abs.* Abby texts back, *He's gross,* followed by the poop emoji.

That night, Clay dreams of Sylvia McLellan. He dreams with some regularity of boarding school—the classic dream that he's unprepared for an exam, plus a more idiosyncratic one that involves a girl named Jenny Pacanowski waiting in her dorm room to have sex with him, while, agitatingly, he's delayed by the task of putting away equipment for the entire lacrosse team—but he's never before dreamed about Sylvia. And the dream Clay has of Sylvia isn't sexual; in fact, within a minute or two of waking, he can't remember what it was about except that it leaves him uneasy. Yet he's not surprised when, four months later, he receives an email from her. They haven't had contact since their graduation in 1991.

Hope you've been well, she writes. *Super-random after all this time, but I'm coming to Chicago for work in April and I was thinking it would be fun to have dinner if you're around.*

After a few volleys, they have settled on a day, a time, and a restaurant near the downtown hotel where she'll stay. She lives in Denver, she tells him, she's an architect, her husband is also an architect but not at her firm, and they're the parents of twin boys who are nine and a girl who's five.

You didn't go into politics, either? Clay types, then he adds the phrase *the dirty business of* between *into* and *politics* to convey that he's kidding, then he deletes the entire question. Her trip to Chicago is three weeks away.

In the spring of 1990, when they were juniors, Clay, Sylvia, and three of their classmates all ran for senior prefect, which was the fancy term used at Bishop Academy for student body president. Their school was in western Massachusetts, and there were a total of seventy-six people in their grade. After Clay and Sylvia tied for first place, a runoff occurred. The exact results were never disclosed, but apparently they were close, so close that the dean of students met with Clay and Sylvia and proposed the following: Because Clay had been their grade prefect for the past three years, and because no girl had ever served as senior prefect—a fact mostly explained by Bishop having switched from all-boys to coed only a decade earlier— Clay would assume the role of senior prefect, but unprecedentedly, another role would be created for Sylvia, that of assistant prefect. Clay would show her the ropes with regard to running Monday and Friday assemblies and serving on the honor council, and in turn, Sylvia would help raise money for senior class activities, especially since, for the first time in Bishop's history, there was a movement afoot to hold a prom.

Clay can still remember sitting in Dean Boede's office, the warm New England afternoon outside the big window, his impending lacrosse practice; he can remember how qualmlessly he accepted this offer and how Sylvia did, too. That night, before everyone was released from Sit-Down Dinner, the headmaster announced the arrangement to the student body, and there was much applause.

Clay had been in a few classes with Sylvia over the years without ever talking to her much, and he thought of her as smart—she had at some point won a prize for an essay written in Latin—as well as quiet and almost definitely a virgin. He'd been surprised when she'd run for prefect. She was tall and thin and had long, straight blond hair, so that she looked hot from behind, but from the front you could see her jutting, rectangular jaw and aquiline nose; besides that, she just didn't carry herself like a hot girl. A week after being elected assistant senior prefect, she also was elected captain of the girls' crew team.

Their senior year played out as Dean Boede had proposed: Sylvia stood on the auditorium stage with Clay during assemblies, she attended honor council meetings, they did indeed hold an all-school prom. The theme was "April in Paris," and the centerpiece was a thirty-foot-high papier-mâché Eiffel Tower, with which Clay personally never had physical contact. By the end of the year, his impression of Sylvia remained favorable. Then again, how much thought did Clay actually give her? He was a reasonably conscientious student, an even more conscientious athlete, and a decent boyfriend to a girl named Meredith Tyler, who was dark-haired and looked hot from both the back and the front; meanwhile, and this was why he'd rate himself merely decent as a boyfriend, he occasionally had sex with Jenny Pacanowski, who also was hot from the back and the front, whom he'd lost his virginity to his sophomore year, who took Ritalin, who'd told him that in first grade she'd repeatedly gotten in trouble for humping the corner of a desk, and who had a boyfriend who'd already graduated from Bishop. Every two or three weeks, Jenny materialized in his dorm room in the middle of the night. There was a rule Clay's mother had about dessert, which was that she couldn't seek it out but if it landed in front of her, she could indulge; not that it would have made his mother proud, but Clay had the same rule about Jenny.

When he, along with Meredith, Jenny, Sylvia, and seventy-two other classmates, graduated on a Sunday morning in early June, Clay was handed his diploma not by the headmaster, as everyone else was, but by his father, who was a trustee of the school and also a graduate. In the fall, Clay started at Yale and Sylvia started at Williams, which made it slightly surprising that during college they never crossed paths, not even on the second-to-last weekend of each October at Head of the Charles.

———

Over email, Clay gave Sylvia a choice of three restaurants—
a tapas place, a pan-Asian place, and a pricey American
bistro—and she picked the bistro; like the others, it's
located a walkable distance between her hotel and the
headquarters of the national bank where he is one of
four executive vice presidents. When he checks in with
the hostess, he can see Sylvia waiting in a booth facing
the entrance, a martini glass in front of her. She stands to
greet him; she's wearing a fitted black cocktail dress, sheer
stockings, and notably high heels, possibly dominatrix-
ish in style; the shoes are unexpected, but good for her.
When they embrace, the heels make her as tall as he is,
which is six-one.

As they sit, he says, "What a nice surprise."

She seems slightly sheepish as she says, "I hope it
didn't seem too out of the blue," and he says, "Not at
all."

In fact, he feels a genuine warmth toward her; he
really did respect her intelligence, her steadiness and sense
of responsibility. There was a controversial situation the
winter of their senior year involving a group of popular
juniors caught drinking together, where some were ex-
pelled and some merely put on probation, and because of
Clay and Sylvia's roles on the honor council, a lot of ill
will was directed toward them. Sylvia's acceptance of the
ill will, the way she acknowledged other people's displea-
sure and didn't make excuses for herself, taught him a
lot. Sitting across the table from her, it occurs to him that
in her present life as an architect, she's probably very
good at what she does, very reliable and professional. It's
also striking how well she's aged. It is, of course, far more

unusual to be tall and slim and blond in the world than it was at Bishop, far more unusual at forty-three than at seventeen. She still has that rectangular, almost horsey jaw, still isn't beautiful, and, especially in her sheepishness, gives off an air of girls' crew captain in uncharacteristically sexy shoes, but she's solidly attractive.

After ordering a beer, he says, "You're in town to meet with a client?"

"A prospective client. But the meeting finished a while ago, which means you're saving me right now from, like, bad room service."

"So why have you skipped all the Bishop reunions?" he says. "Don't tell me it's because you can resist the pull of nostalgia."

"I actually went to the twenty-fifth, but *you* weren't there."

"That's the only one I bailed on." Their twenty-fifth was last May, less than a year ago. He says, "My divorce was being finalized and—" He breaks off. "I'm sure you can imagine. I didn't feel too celebratory."

"Well, I hadn't avoided them on purpose," she says. "I'd meant to go before, but something always came up. At our fifth reunion, my mom was having surgery, at our tenth, Nelson and I—my husband—I think we were in Europe, and I don't remember the rest. But there was always a reason. I'm sorry about your divorce, by the way. I know that's tough."

He sighs. "Hopefully, the worst is behind us. It was fairly amicable, as these things go."

"Have you been in Chicago all this time?"

"I did a stint in New York before HBS. But I've been

here for fifteen years, so, hey, only fifteen more until I'm a real midwesterner."

"You grew up in Connecticut, didn't you?" she says. "There's so much I can't remember in my daily life, like where I left my keys and what night my kids' Cub Scouts meetings are, but I'm afraid my memories of Bishop are weirdly intact."

"That's impressive," he says. "I'm from Darien." He doesn't know where she grew up, which she seems to recognize, because she taps her chest and says, "Burlington, Vermont."

"And how long have you guys been in Denver?"

"Eight years. My in-laws are there, so that's a double-edged sword." As the waitress delivers his beer, Sylvia holds up her glass, which is still a third full and contains two green olives on a toothpick, and says to the waitress, "Another gin martini?" Then she tilts her glass toward him and says, "Cheers." As they clink, she asks, "Which of our classmates are you in touch with?"

"Warrington Russell's been trying to persuade a bunch of us to meet at his lodge up in Alaska some summer, have a week of fly-fishing, but we'll see. Coordinating the calendars of five men in their forties is like herding cats. What about you?"

"Laurie Dixon was in Denver a couple years ago, and we had lunch, but I've been pretty lame overall. That's why it was good to catch up with everyone at the reunion." She takes a sip and says, "A lot of your family went to Bishop, right? So you must naturally run into people."

Is there some subtext to this comment? He isn't sure.

He says, "Yeah, both my older brothers. And my dad, too, and my uncle." There's a pause, and he says, "How'd you end up at Bishop? Were you from a family where boarding school was the default?"

"My parents were both professors, and neither of them had gone away to school, but some of their students had. I was attending a not great public middle school, and when the teachers floated the idea of my skipping a grade, I applied to Bishop instead. Did you hear that Dean Boede died?"

It's still early, and it might be a little easier if Clay himself had consumed more alcohol, but this feels like the right moment. He clears his throat. "I want to say—I'm not sure if this is why you got in touch—obviously, if it is, I respect it—but after Trump was elected, in the past few months, I've been thinking about our time at Bishop, and I want to apologize." The expression on her face is a little weird, as if maybe she's amused, but he perseveres. "I guess we'll never know the results of that runoff, but I'd be willing to bet I lost and you won. And even if it was a different time, even if I wasn't the one who came up with the plan, what happened was completely sexist. I just want to say I recognize that now and I'm sorry."

She's watching him intently, still with that amused-seeming expression, and she says, "Is that why you think I suggested having dinner? To extract an apology?"

He hesitates, then says, "I'm not faulting you if you did. I get it."

"Hmm." She looks to the side for a few seconds, at other diners, and she seems to consider his comments, then she makes eye contact again. "I'll tell you something about that stuff at Bishop," she says. "In the first round, before the runoff, I voted for you. Frankly, I probably thought I'd make a better senior prefect, but I also thought back then that it was conceited or indecorous or something to vote for myself. Did you vote for yourself?"

"Yes." He adds, "It was a competition."

"No, I know. You *should* have voted for yourself. I should have, too. But it's just funny because if I had, we wouldn't have tied and I bet Dean Boede wouldn't have come up with his boneheaded plan. He was your football coach, right? And he clearly favored you. At the same time, I learned an important lesson from all that, which was to be my own advocate and if I came off as immodest, so be it. And you have to figure that out at some point. Or at least if you're a woman, you do, or not a white man. Architecture is totally an old boys' field—the vast majority of partners at firms are men, and a lot of times if a woman *is* a partner, it's a woman without kids."

"Well, if that's the case," Clay says, "you're welcome." He can tell immediately that she didn't like the joke—she raises her eyebrows and purses her lips in a sort of fake-pleased way—and he strongly wishes he hadn't made it.

"Just to be clear," she says, "I'm not brushing off what happened like it was no big deal and I'm so easygoing. It was appalling. It's just that I worked through my issues about it a long time ago. For me, it's appalling, but it's also old news."

"Fair enough," he says.

There's a silence, then, slowly, she says, "Out of curiosity, before our country decided to elect an unhinged narcissist over an intelligent, experienced, qualified woman—before that, had it really never occurred to you that the senior prefect thing was sexist?"

The narrowness of the margin of error here, combined with the high likelihood of his screwing up—it reminds him of marriage counseling. He, too, speaks slowly. "If you're asking if I was introspective about it at the time, no. I wish I had been, but it'd be a lie."

"When the tape was released about grabbing women by the pussy and all these men suddenly said, 'As a father of girls, I object'—was that how you felt? Like, I'm cool with him saying terrible things about Mexican people and Muslims, but this is too much?"

"I was never cool with Trump's racism."

"Are you a Republican?" Her accusatory tone, her clear antipathy—he's simultaneously eager to move himself out of their line of fire and struck by a detached awareness of how different she's become. He was initially lulled, misled, by her relatively unchanged appearance, but perhaps she's hardly the same person at all. Because it's not just that the Bishop version of Sylvia wouldn't have directed this sort of hostility at him; it's that he doesn't believe such hostility existed in her.

"I've supported people in both parties," he says. "I take it you're a straight-ticket voter?"

"I guess it shouldn't surprise me," she says, and she seems less angry than pensive. "If you're not in the one percent, you must be close. So why wouldn't you be conservative? If not you, who?"

Is Sylvia McLellan now a social justice warrior? That seems a bit preposterous, in her cocktail dress and her dominatrix shoes, staying in what's probably a four-hundred-dollar-a-night hotel.

Evenly, he says, "I'd describe myself as an independent. I kind of liked Bernie."

She raises her eyebrows again, and says, "Maybe that shouldn't surprise me, either."

Mercifully, this is when the waitress appears to take their order. He asks for roasted chicken, and she orders braised beef, and when the waitress leaves, he says, "I know I'll have entrée envy, but another thing about getting older is, I seriously think I get meat hangovers. With red meat, at least. But I salute you."

And at first, he believes he's successfully diverted her. They move on to talking about various diets, then about their respective exercise routines (he plays tennis a few times a week, while she tries to hike and ski but usually just works out on an elliptical machine in her basement), and she evinces interest in his Fitbit, which he removes and hands to her. Then they discuss where they've traveled over the years. But just after the waitress has cleared their plates, then taken an order for a cappuccino from him and another martini for her, Sylvia says, "I'll tell you why I really called you. You know, in the spirit of honesty you showed."

There's something both rehearsed-seeming and sarcastic in her tone, something not reassuring. But as she continues speaking, she sounds more sincere. "My husband was laid off almost a year ago. Even with Nelson out of work, we're okay—we can pay our mortgage. But we're careful about money in a way we never had to be before. We don't go out for nice dinners anymore, we stop and think before we sign the kids up for activities, even as we're trying to shield them from the situation, and who knows if *that's* a good idea? Grace is too young, but maybe it'd be better if we told the twins. Anyway, Nelson now tries to convince me it's acceptable to give a ten-dollar Target gift card as a birthday present to their classmates, and it's definitely not—you're better off giving some shitty toy where at least the other parents don't know the price. But I digress." Sylvia sips from her glass. "Given that Nelson isn't working, you might think he'd use his time to, like, make healthy family dinners, or exercise, or clean the garage. You know, life gives you lemons. Instead, he spends every day wearing this hideous pair of black track pants with two orange stripes down the side and playing online video games. Maybe I should be grateful he's not looking at porn, or maybe he is looking at porn and telling me he's playing video games—at some point, I don't know if there's much of a difference."

"I'm sorry to hear all that," Clay says.

"We're about to get to the part that has to do with you," she says. "If you're wondering."

Again, this does not reassure him.

"When we were at Bishop, I had a huge crush on you," she says. "Which I assume you knew."

In fact, he is stunned. He says, "On me?"

She laughs and then, perhaps in a parody of a southern belle, tilts her face up and bats her eyelashes. She says, "On little old me?"

But this really isn't what he was expecting. He was imagining she was about to ask for some sort of job referral for her husband, or for an investment in a business they're starting. And never at Bishop, not once, did it occur to him that she was interested in him in that way.

In her normal voice, she says, "Of course I liked you.

Think about it. You were this good-looking, confident guy, you were nice to me, and we were around each other a lot." She's managing to make these remarks feel less like a compliment than a confession, possibly a reprimand. "Sometimes after we had those evening meetings with Dean Boede, I'd go back to my room and lie on my bed and cry because I loved you so much. I wanted to touch you so badly, and I wanted you to touch me, and there was nothing I could do to make it happen. It was like flirting was a language I didn't speak. Plus, you had your whole harem of girls. Not just Meredith but Jenny, too, right? And I knew I wasn't in the same league with either of them, I knew that liking you was liking above my station. But here you were, this eighteen-year-old lacrosse player, and your hands and your forearms were so beautiful I almost couldn't stand it. When I think of Bishop, I probably should think about my well-rounded education or my time rowing on the river, but mostly I just remember feeling desperate with longing." Although she's now smiling, he has the impression that the smile is not for him but for her own younger self. And it's still unclear what her ultimate point is, so he waits, saying nothing.

"I didn't really have a meeting in Chicago," she continues. "I came here to go on a date with you. You wouldn't know it was a date, but I would. I'd dress up, and we'd go to the kind of restaurant that Nelson and I don't go to anymore, *this* kind of restaurant." She gestures with one arm. "I'd drink a little too much, not that I'm three sheets to the wind or anything. I'm maybe one sheet to the wind. But I'd Google-Imaged you, so I knew you were still cute, and I also knew you were divorced."

Is she finished? He waits a few seconds to make sure before saying, "Just so you know, I'm seeing someone. A woman named Jane."

"Oh, that doesn't matter," Sylvia says. "This is a pretend date, a fake date. I wasn't hoping we'd end up in bed. For one thing, I don't think I could live with the guilt, and for another, childbirth wrecked my body. I can hide it when my clothes are on, but having the twins ruined my vagina, and having my daughter ruined my butt. Have you ever heard of anal fissures?"

Is this a rhetorical question? After a pause, he says, "Yes, I've heard of them."

"Have you ever had one?" She's as blasé as if she's asking if he's ever tasted coconut water.

He shakes his head.

"The comparison people make is to a paper cut on your asshole," she says. "As for the rest of my parts down there, I'll spare you the details, but suffice it to say that other women sometimes tell me they didn't know it's possible to give birth to twins vaginally, and, having done it, I'm not sure it is." She smirks, then holds her glass aloft. "Live and learn."

This, to him, is her ugliest moment yet—the purity of her cynicism, the unapologeticness of her vulgarity. Did she change gradually, little by little, or all at once?

"I was in the room when my ex-wife gave birth to our daughter," Clay says. "I'm not some nineteen-fifties man who's totally ignorant about the mechanics of the female body."

She's still smiling as she says, "Should I congratulate you for that?"

He takes care to keep his voice calm, not to match her

antipathy, when he says, "At the same time, here's a friendly tip for you, if you're trying to reenter the dating pool. I wouldn't recommend bringing up the topic of anal fissures."

She doesn't seem at all embarrassed; if anything, she remains amused as she says, "I guess I haven't done a good job of explaining myself. I'm not planning to cheat on Nelson. This—tonight—it was an experiment, but I knew very quickly that it was a failed experiment. You're still good-looking, I'll grant you that. But you're so boring! You probably found me boring, and I *was* boring tonight, but I was feeding off your boringness. Isn't it weird how I was tormented as a teenager by a person who grew up into a banker who talks incessantly about his Fitbit?"

Their waitress is nearby, and he catches her eye and makes the check-requesting gesture. Then he extracts a credit card from his wallet and, when the waitress brings over the small leather folder, passes her the card without looking at the bill.

"Did I offend you?" Sylvia asks. "I didn't mean to. I was trying to be factual."

He says nothing—what's the point?—and after a few seconds, she adds, "For all his faults, Nelson does make me laugh. He's very funny. And I think a sense of humor is the single most endearing quality a person can have. Do you agree?"

Apparently, this isn't a rhetorical question, either. They look at each other, and he says, "Sure."

"Sure? That's it?"

"It seems like we've both said what we have to say to each other tonight."

Another silence ensues, a long silence, while they await the return of the bill, and at last Sylvia says, "So your daughter's, what, a high school freshman? Or a sophomore?"

"Abby's a freshman," he says.

"Is she athletic like you?"

This is how their last moments in the restaurant conclude, with a conversation that in tone and content is the one he'd anticipated having with her in the first place. It's a reminder that, probably, nothing is wrong with Sylvia, nothing diagnosable. She just turned out weird and bitter.

On the street, under the dark city sky, before they walk in opposite directions, Sylvia says, "Thanks so much for dinner."

Normally, he'd hug her again, or perhaps kiss her on the cheek. And it feels odd to do nothing—as odd as it would have to split the check, *not* to pay for her—so he extends his hand, and as they shake, she smirks again. She says, "Farewell to thee in the perilous storm," which is a line from the Bishop hymn, a song that even now, maybe especially now, he finds deeply moving. Without question, his moral code was molded more by the ideals of Bishop than by those of his parents. This is why he doesn't care how paternalistic, how sexist, how *Republican* he sounds to Sylvia when he says, as his parting words, "Is it really necessary for you to poison that, too?"

They'd exchanged phone numbers over email, and she'd texted him around noon, to confirm dinner. Therefore, her number but not her name are in the Contacts of his cellphone, and when his phone rings just after eleven, while he is lying in bed watching television, he has no idea at first who it might be. But, because he is a parent, he answers.

Immediately, Sylvia says, "Do you remember that kid Bruno in the grade below ours? The day after our prefect announcement, he staged a one-person picket outside the headmaster's house to try to get them to release the final vote tally. And I thought he was a freak."

Carefully—it's difficult to discern whether her mood is more ruminative or combative—Clay says, "I do remember Bruno."

"The truth is that when Dean Boede handed you the election, I didn't think it was that weird," Sylvia says. "At the time, I was good at not getting what I wanted. Plus, I was sort of shy. I'd never have run for senior prefect if my crew teammates hadn't encouraged me. So I thought, Okay, this makes sense. I'll be the sidekick. When I told my parents, they were confused, and I could tell they thought it was strange I didn't know the vote tally. But they didn't push it, and they were proud of me for being assistant prefect. It wasn't until I described what had happened to my college friends that anyone ever said, What the fuck? They were like, Why did no one protest? Why did no adults intervene?"

Partly to humor her and partly because he believes it, Clay says, "So it was all of us *except* Bruno who were the freaks."

"Good old Bruno," Sylvia says, and her voice sounds warmer than it did at the restaurant, though he'd be foolish to entirely trust her. "The other thing," she says, "is that even though I made fun of you for not knowing sexism existed before last fall, I was shocked when Hillary lost and Trump won. I'm still shocked. Every single day, every time I see in the news what Trump has said or done, I literally can't believe it."

"Me neither."

"Apparently, that's very white of us—being shocked by the election. Do you have any black friends?"

"Sure," he says.

"Who?"

"A guy I play tennis with, a guy in my building. Do you want their names?"

"I don't have any black friends," she says. "I know people, obviously, but there's no one I hang out with. Although, do I have friends, period? I work fifty hours a week, and I have three kids." They are both quiet, and she adds, "In general, I have no desire to ever have another conversation about Hillary Clinton, to debate the role her gender played. I'm not sure I want to have *any* conversation about sexism. If someone doesn't see that gender played a huge role, why would I waste my time trying to convince them?"

"That's reasonable."

"But I also can't help seeing the election as a metaphor. It turns out that democracies aren't that stable, and neither are marriages. And I'm so fucking confused! I didn't think I'd be this confused when I was forty-three."

"Well," he says, "I'm divorced. It goes without saying that this isn't exactly what I had planned."

"I thought I had my act together," she says. "I have my job, I have my family, we're all, knock on wood, pretty healthy. There was this story I told myself, that growing up I'd been the awkward good girl, the responsible student, and I'd missed out socially but in the long term I'd come out ahead. So it was all fine, it all comes out in the wash, or whatever it is people say. I thought I was finished being the teenager who lay in her dorm room and felt racked with misery, wanting things she couldn't have. But something came loose inside me, something got dislodged, and I *am* still that teenager. In a way, it started even before Nelson got laid off—it started when this dad at my kids' school was killed in a motorcycle accident. It was awful. His children were in fourth and seventh grade at the time. And you'd think that would make me treasure my own family, make me grateful for what I have, but instead, it made me sort of reckless and crazy. Like, who knows what will happen to any of us, so why shouldn't I enjoy myself in the way I've never been good at? Why shouldn't I get to have fun, too? I've never done drugs, I've never even really *seen* drugs, but recently I've wondered, Should I try to find some cocaine? Or Ecstasy? Because I want a hit of something—I want some kind of lift, something to break up the monotony. What's maybe weirdest about having reverted to my teenage longings is that this time around, I don't know what they're for. Back then, they were for you, but what am I so desperate for now? What can I get or do that will make me feel better instead of worse? That's why I came to Chicago and pretended we were on a date. I just wanted something."

"Before you try street drugs," Clay says, "have you talked to your husband about any of this? Or to a therapist?"

"I know I sound like a horrible wife, and maybe I am—the part of me that looks at Nelson and thinks, Pull yourself together. But at the same time, I *am* sympathetic and I recognize how much pain he's in, and how, as a man, his self-worth is more tied up in providing for our family than mine is. It's easy to pretend that if I got fired, I'd train for a triathlon and declutter our house, but I'd probably just sit around on my ass, too, being depressed." She pauses. "I didn't answer your question, did I? We sort of talk about it. And I went to a therapist a few times, but she wasn't very smart."

"This is just my two cents, but you don't seem like a person who wants out of your marriage," he says. "Maybe you will eventually, but you don't now."

"Really? Why not?" She seems genuinely interested.

He pauses, then says, "The anal fissure stuff—you put it out there that we were on a date, but you immediately followed up with that. It was like you were sex-proofing the situation."

She laughs. "That's an intriguing theory. But there's no version of tonight that would have played out with us hooking up, is there?"

"The possibility of two people becoming physically involved generally hinges on both of them being open to it."

"Oh, come on. That's such a cop-out. Would you have slept with me?"

He thinks, *Based on your appearance, sure. Based on your behavior, no.* Aloud, he says, "I know you'll think I'm dodging the question, but it's impossible to say. It's like the butterfly effect."

"I'd have been okay with making out, I think," she says. "I never kissed a Bishop boy, not even once, so I'd be able to cross that off my bucket list at the ripe old age of forty-three. Can you believe I graduated from high school without kissing anyone? It seems like it shouldn't be possible."

"Like giving birth to twins vaginally," he says, and she laughs again and says, "Touché."

"For what it's worth," he says, "everyone feels weird about their aging body. It's not a crime not to look like you're eighteen. Anyway, you're attractive. I assume you know that by now."

She is silent, and he wonders if, again, he's misstepped. If he has, well—fuck her. She didn't need to call him again. Then she sighs, sadly rather than resentfully. She says, "I once heard that smart women want to be told they're pretty and pretty women want to be told they're smart. And the depressing part is that I think I agree. What did you say your girlfriend's name is?"

"See?" he says. "You just did it again. I told you you're attractive and you brought up my girlfriend."

This time, she laughs so heartily and authentically that, in a visceral way, it takes him back to their senior year at Bishop; it's a laugh he'd forgotten about but recognizes instantly. (Oh, the passage of time! The twenty-six years that have elapsed, the green afternoon outside Dean Boede's office! The irretrievability of his youth, the Bishop hymn, the blow jobs he used to get from Jenny Pacanowski.)

He says, "For the record, I really had no idea, none at all, that you were interested in me at Bishop. Maybe part of getting what you want is asking for it."

"Said like a man."

"That doesn't make it wrong."

The pause that ensues is the longest yet between them. He thinks about the distance between Wilmette, where his condo is, and her hotel and how many minutes it would take to drive there at this hour. (Thirty?) The thought is mostly but not completely speculative, and it's hard to imagine that she's not thinking about the same thing.

What she says when she finally speaks is "Did you cheat on your wife?"

"We were both involved with other people."

"Who did it first?"

"She did, although she'd say I was checked out of the marriage by then."

"Are you relieved or bummed out that you're divorced?"

"Yes."

She laughs. "Do *you* feel confused and desperate?"

"Sometimes."

She says, "Now that we're friends again—we're friends again, right?"

"I hope so."

"Now that we're friends again, *have* you ever had an anal fissure? Because they really are insanely painful."

"I wasn't lying," he says. "I haven't."

"Nelson once had hemorrhoids at the same time I had an anal fissure, and he said we should start a band called Sylvia McLellan and the Buttcheeks." After a pause, she says, "I guess you had to be there." There's another pause—some shift seems to have occurred, some definitive understanding that they will not see each other again tonight, which is allowing them both to capitulate to their own tiredness—and she says, "I shouldn't have said you were boring. It was rude, but it was also untrue. I appreciate your psychological insights."

Alone in his bedroom, he smiles. "Thank you, Sylvia."

Knowing he's not going to her hotel makes it easier for him to settle into an uncomplicated and nostalgic affection for her. Will they stay in touch? Will they ever cross paths again? Possibly at a reunion, but otherwise, it seems highly unlikely.

"Did my call wake you up?" she asks, and it's the combination of how sincere her concern seems with how belated it is that amuses him.

He says, "I was watching TV."

She yawns audibly. "What show?"

He tells her the name; it's a cable drama that's been airing for a few years, though he's only halfway through the first season.

"Oh, I've heard that's good," she says, and her voice is now so drowsy, so intimate with impending sleep, that it's as if she is lying in the bed next to him. She says, "Maybe that's what Nelson and I will watch next."

Acknowledgments

For supporting me as I write the books I want to write, for excelling at what they do, and for being so much fun to work with, I am deeply grateful to my agent, Jennifer Rudolph Walsh; my editor, Jennifer Hershey; and my publicist, Maria Braeckel. I thank the many other wonderful people I work with at WME, including Raffaella DeAngelis, Tracy Fisher, Elizabeth Sheinkman, Alicia Gordon, Erin Conroy, Jill Gillett, Suzanne Gluck, Eve Attermann, Eric Zohn, Alicia Everett, Sabrina Giglio, Becky Chalsen, and Erika Niven, and the equally wonderful people I work with at Random House, including Gina Centrello, Avideh Bashirrad, Theresa Zoro, Christine Mykityshyn, Sally Marvin, Leigh Marchant, Susan Kamil, Sanyu Dillon, Caitlin McCaskey, Anastasia Whalen, Khusbu Bhakta, Erin Kane, Benjamin Dreyer, Jessica Yung, Janet Wygal, Bonnie Thompson, Jessica Bonet, Stephanie Reddaway, Paolo Pepe, Robbin Schiff, and Liz Eno. Marianne Velmans and Patsy Irwin at Transworld in the U.K. look out for me and my writing from across an ocean. A book publication is always a collaborative act, and I am so lucky that these are my collaborators.

In addition, I thank the smart and patient editors who originally shepherded some of these stories into print: above all, Willing Davidson, as well as Scott Stossel, Maria Streshinsky, David Rowell, and Elizabeth Merrick.

I thank the people who read early drafts and/or helped me sort out specific facts: Nick Arvin, Matt Bodie and Rebecca Hollander-Blumoff, Dave Carlson, Sheena MJ Cook, emily m. danforth, Susanna Daniel, Matthew Klam, Grace Lee, Consuelo and Ian Macpherson, Edward McPherson, Maile Meloy, Emily Miller, Annie Morriss, Sasha Polonsky Tulgan, Shauna Seliy, Malena Watrous, and Jennifer Weiner. Beth Guterman Chu, who knows much more about classical music than I do, actually wrote many of the sentences in the emails in "Plausible Deniability." Andrea Denny is a delightful person with whom to discuss suburban life. For being good sports about my books and for occasionally letting me steal details when they're so juicy or perfect I can't resist, I thank my parents, Betsy and Paul Sittenfeld, as well as my siblings and their spouses: Tiernan Sittenfeld and Darren Speece; Josephine Sittenfeld and Thad Russell; and P. G. Sittenfeld and Sarah Coyne Sittenfeld. I thank my husband, Matt, and our children for being my true story.

My beloved friend Samuel Park was the first reader of many of these stories. Sam died in April 2017. It's not the same to be a writer without his brilliant, witty, and encouraging feedback, and it's not the same to be a person in the world without his friendship.

About the Author

Some of **Curtis Sittenfeld**'s short stories have appeared in the *New Yorker* and *Esquire*. She is the author of the word-of-mouth bestseller *American Wife*, which was longlisted for the Orange Prize, as was her first novel, *Prep*, a *New York Times* bestseller. *Sisterland*, her fourth novel, was a Richard & Judy Book Club pick, and her most recent *Sunday Times* bestseller was *Eligible*, a contemporary retelling of *Pride and Prejudice*. She is married, with two young children, and lives in St Louis in the American Mid-West.

Visit her website, www.curtissittenfeld.com